I0762107

PRAISE FOR KRISTINE KATHRYN RUSCH'S DIVING UNIVERSE

"The Diving Universe, conceived by Hugo-Award winning author Kristine [Kathryn] Rusch is a refreshingly new and fleshed out realm of sci-fi action and adventure."

ASTROGUYZ

"Kristine Kathryn Rusch is best known for her Retrieval Artist series, so maybe you've missed her Diving Universe series. If so, it's high time to remedy that oversight."

ANALOG

"This is classic sci-fi, a well-told tale of dangerous exploration. The firstperson narration makes the reader an eye witness to the vast, silent realms of deep space, where even the smallest error will bring disaster. Compellingly human and technically absorbing, the suspense builds to fevered intensity, culminating in an explosive yet plausible conclusion."

RT BOOK REVIEWS (TOP PICK) ON DIVING INTO THE WRECK

"Rusch delivers a page-turning space adventure while contemplating the ethics of scientists and governments working together on future tech."

PUBLISHERS WEEKLY ON DIVING INTO THE WRECK

"Rusch's handling of the mystery and adventure is stellar, and the whole tale proves quite entertaining."

BOOKLIST ONLINE ON DIVING INTO THE WRECK

"The technicalities in Boss' story are beautifully played.... She's real, flawed, and interesting.... Read the book. It is very good."

SFFWORLD ON DIVING INTO THE WRECK

"Kristine Kathryn Rusch's Diving into the Wreck is exactly what the sf genre needs to get more readers...and to keep the readers the genre already has."

ELITIST BOOK REVIEWS ON DIVING INTO THE WRECK

"Rusch keeps the science accessible, the cultures intriguing, and the characters engaging. For anyone needing to add to their science fiction library, keep an eye out for this."

SPECULATIVE FICTION EXAMINER ON CITY OF RUINS

"Rusch's latest addition to her Diving series features a strong, capable female heroine and a vividly imagined far-future universe. Blending fast-paced action with an exploration of the nature of friendship and the ethics of scientific discoveries, this tale should appeal to Rusch's readers and fans of space opera."

LIBRARY JOURNAL ON BONEYARDS

"Rusch follows Diving into the Wreck and City of Ruins with another fast-paced novel of the far future... [Rusch's] sensibilities will endear this book to readers looking for a light, quick space adventure with strong female protagonists."

PUBLISHERS WEEKLY ON BONEYARDS

"Filled with well-defined characters who confront a variety of ethical and moral dilemmas, Rusch's third Diving novel is classic space opera, with richly detailed worldbuilding and lots of drama."

RT BOOK REVIEWS ON BONEYARDS

"...a fabulous outer space thriller that rotates perspective between the divers, the Alliance and to a lesser degree the Empire. Action-packed and filled with twists yet allowing the reader to understand the motives of the key players, Skirmishes is another intelligent exciting voyage into the Rusch Diving universe."

THE MIDWEST BOOK REVIEW ON SKIRMISHES

"A combination of first-person and third-person narrative and flashback segments makes this a complex and compelling story. It's like having three tales in one, with an added peek into the bad guys' activities, all of them intriguing, classic science fiction. It leaves the reader eager to explore this universe again and see what will happen next with these characters."

RT BOOK REVIEWS ON SKIRMISHES

"A skillful blend of science fiction and murder mystery which keeps ratcheting up the stakes."

WORLDS WITHOUT END ON THE FALLS

"[The Runabout] is so good, it will make you want to read the other stories."

SFREVU ON THE RUNABOUT

"Amazing character construction, building a plot that riveted me almost from the moment it began. I will now absolutely have to read the preceding titles and I cannot wait to see what will come as a result of *The Runabout*."

TANGENT ONLINE ON THE RUNABOUT

"By mixing cerebral and investigative elements, emotional character segments, and the adrenaline of action, Rusch tells a complete yet varied tale that will please science fiction readers looking for something different from the usual fare."

PUBLISHERS WEEKLY ON SEARCHING FOR THE FLEET

"One of the most amazing science fiction series in recent years now has an exciting new installment."

ASTROGUYZ ON SEARCHING FOR THE FLEET

THE COURT-MARTIAL OF THE RENEGAT RENEGADES

A DIVING UNIVERSE NOVEL

KRISTINE KATHRYN RUSCH

The Court-Martial of the Renegat Renegades

Published by WMG Publishing

First published in *Asimov's Science Fiction,* September/October 2022 and November/December 2022

Cover design by Allyson Longueira/WMG Publishing

ISBN-13 (trade paperback): 978-1-56146-845-4

ISBN-13 (hardcover): 978-1-56146-872-0

THE DIVING SERIES (READING ORDER)

Diving into the Wreck: A Diving Novel

City of Ruins: A Diving Novel

Becalmed: A Diving Universe Novella

The Application of Hope: A Diving Universe Novella

Boneyards: A Diving Novel

Skirmishes: A Diving Novel

The Runabout: A Diving Novel

The Falls: A Diving Universe Novel

Searching for the Fleet: A Diving Novel

The Spires of Denon: A Diving Universe Novella

The Renegat: A Diving Universe Novel

Escaping Amnthra: A Diving Universe Novella

The Court-Martial of the Renegat Renegades

Thieves: A Diving Novel

Squishy's Teams: A Diving Universe Novel

The Chase: A Diving Novel

Maelstrom: A Diving Universe Novella

ALSO BY KRISTINE KATHRYN RUSCH

THE RETRIEVAL ARTIST SERIES

The Disappeared

Extremes

Consequences

Buried Deep

Paloma

Recovery Man

The Recovery Man's Bargain

Duplicate Effort

The Possession of Paavo Deshin

Anniversary Day

Blowback

A Murder of Clones

Search & Recovery

The Peyti Crisis

Vigilantes

Starbase Human

Masterminds

The Impossibles

The Retrieval Artist

The Fey Series

THE ORIGINAL BOOKS OF THE FEY

The Sacrifice: Book One of the Fey

The Changeling: Book Two of the Fey

The Rival: Book Three of the Fey

The Resistance: Book Four of the Fey

Victory: Book Five of the Fey

THE BLACK THRONE

The Black Queen: Book One of the Black Throne

The Black King: Book Two of the Black Throne

THE QAVNERIAN PROTECTORATE

The Reflection on Mount Vitaki: Prequel to the Qavnerian Protectorate

The Kirilli Matter: The First Book of the Qavnerian Protectorate

Barkson's Journey: The Second Book of the Qavnerian Protectorate

(coming 2023)

WRITING AS KRIS NELSCOTT

THE SMOKEY DALTON SERIES

A Dangerous Road

Smoke-Filled Rooms

Thin Walls

Stone Cribs

War at Home

Days of Rage

Street Justice

And

Protectors

THE COURT-MARTIAL OF THE RENEGAT RENEGADES

ONE

A hand slapped the side of her desk, jarring Lucinda Arias awake. She had drool on her left cheek, which she wiped off with a knuckle that wasn't entirely clean. She couldn't remember the last time she took a shower.

"Hey, Arias," a male voice said near her. "Snap to."

God, she hated that old phrase. And the fact that someone had used it meant she was dealing with the Old Man.

She blinked, wiped off her mouth, wished her hair was combed, and sat up. The office was mostly empty. It was a cavernous room that no one had bothered to fix up. Some of the protective tiles had fallen off the ceiling when she was a young lawyer, and they hadn't been replaced in decades.

The office also had a distinctive odor of burned coffee and human sweat. Sometimes she thought that scent was baked in. She really didn't smell the coffee right now, and she suspected the smell of sweat came from her.

The nighttime lights were on, which hadn't caused her to fall asleep —nope, the entire place had been bathed in light when she had returned from court—but the nighttime lighting had probably made her sleep so deeply she had forgotten where she was.

Of course, she slept here often, catching a nap on one of the ancient uncomfortable couches scattered around the large room. She wasn't the only lawyer who occasionally slept here. Just at the edge of her line of sight were the dirty bottoms of a pair of men's dress shoes, poking up on the arm of the closest couch. She didn't lean over to see who was sleeping there, because she really didn't care. She was too concerned with sorting out her own mental state.

Usually, she fell asleep here in the middle of a case, not at the end. She had gone to her desk—which she only used to store things like her proprietary devices and actual physical evidence—and sat down to officially record her side of the case. She'd won, which made the closing assessment a lot more fun to compile, but her win had come at the cost of nearly two weeks of three hours of sleep per night.

She hadn't realized how tired she was until right now, when it felt like her eyes couldn't get unglued.

And in front of the Old Man.

"Sir," she said, rubbing the inside of her eyes with her thumbs. "Sorry about my appearance—"

"I don't give a crap about your appearance, Arias. I need you on this." A proprietary tablet appeared in front of her.

God, another classified case. The kind she would have to guard with her life. The kind she would have to be careful to touch the right controls, because otherwise she would delete everything of importance. The kind that would eat her life just like this last one had.

"Sir," she said. "I still have to close the file on the Herron case."

She didn't look up at him, not yet, because she wasn't sure she could mask the irritation. Lawyers weren't supposed to work this hard once they reached her level. She was the best in the Starbase Sigma office, with a higher percentage of wins at her age than the Old Man had.

She deserved time off. She deserved some kind of commendation.

She deserved…

Ah, hell, he knew that. And he wasn't going to care. She could almost mouth his next words with him.

"Have your second chair do it. What was his name? Stevens?"

"Stephan, Sir," she said. "And that's his first name. His last name is Rorrbutan."

"Right," the Old Man said in his most dry voice, "because that's easy to remember."

She glanced over at him in surprise, no longer caring how she looked. The Old Man was sarcastic and difficult, but he rarely insulted his team, especially since he had handpicked them based on their skill. He believed in all of them.

But the Old Man looked exhausted too. Arias had no idea how old he actually was. Marciela Kublis, who had been in the office nearly fifty years (please God, don't let her be in the office fifty years) said he had been called the Old Man from the moment he took the job, back when he had his own hair.

Hair was the Old Man's only vanity. He had thick silver hair, layered and styled to perfection. His hair wouldn't have become a joke if he hadn't brought the whole office in on the decision-making, fifteen years before Arias arrived, trying to figure out what kind of hair would most impress the panels of judges the cases were most often heard before.

The joke got carried down through prosecutor after prosecutor, even as the older ones—the ones who had actually been consulted—left. And through it all, the Old Man remained consistent.

He displayed no vanity anywhere else, or he would have worked on his face. It had deep worry lines carved around his mouth, nose, and eyes. The skin had wrinkled everywhere else, rather like nanobits that had started to decay.

As the worry lines around his eyes grew deeper, they bulged forward, making him seem even more intense than he was—and he was very, very intense.

Especially the way he looked right now.

He waved the tablet at her. "We got it. The dog of a case. And you're prosecuting."

The dog of a case. She blinked again, trying to remember. There had been some discussion in the office about upcoming cases, but she had ignored most of it, too busy in the Herron case to pay attention to anything else.

"Sir?" she asked.

"The *Renegat*," he said. "We get to try the bastards for mutiny."

TWO

Mutiny.

Sounded straightforward and it usually was. Some idiot got it in his head that the command structure onboard a Fleet vessel not only didn't apply to him, but it also shouldn't apply to anyone else. Or that he knew better than everyone else how to run the ship, even though he was—pick your poison—a navigator or a med tech or (once that she knew of) a chef in the captain's mess.

But the *Renegat* case: there was nothing straightforward about it.

The ship had limped back to the Fleet with only a third of her original crew. Someone had overthrown the captain, but there was a dispute as to whom and whether that person was still on the ship.

And then there was the sympathy factor.

The survivors of the *Renegat* had traveled back to the Fleet in a damaged ship, enduring at least one battle with a hostile force, and arrived, against all odds, just as the ship had been on its last legs.

Not to mention the time factor.

The *Renegat* had either gotten trapped in foldspace or discovered some kind of new foldspace bubble (depending on which expert was talking about it), and the crew lost one hundred years. Foldspace made even the most jaded Fleet officer nervous. It was a convenient way to travel—crossing what some compared to a fold in a blanket—but it was fraught with dangers. The *Renegat* had encountered one of them.

The rescue of the *Renegat* had been dramatic and traumatic, and half of the Fleet thought the survivors, no matter what they had done, should be allowed to retire somewhere nice and neat and on land.

Arias was one of those people who thought the survivors should just vanish onto some about-to-be closed sector base never to be worried about again. But she didn't dare admit that to her boss.

Although he was giving her the strangest look she had ever seen, as if he was gauging her reaction. So she'd give him as negative a reaction as she could without being political about it.

"It's a dog of a case, sir," she said, repeating his words back to him. "It'll mess up the win record of anyone who takes it."

The wrinkles in his face smoothed out ever so slightly, almost as if he were going to smile and then thought the better of it.

"So," he said, "you think whoever takes the case will lose."

The sleeping person on the nearby couch snorted. Arias couldn't tell if that was a snore or a chortle. Not that it mattered. Her reaction was the same. A sad feeling of resignation, one that forced her to put her real opinion on the record—at least with the Old Man.

"Yes, sir," she said. "Based on what I know, I think whoever takes this case will lose."

"And what do you know?" he asked, starting one of those lawyerly dances.

"That everyone who travels with the Fleet is terrified of two things," she said. "Going backwards and getting trapped in foldspace. The survivors of the *Renegat* experienced both."

"We're trying in front of judges, not a jury," the Old Man said.

She knew he was making an argument, but she hated that he stated the obvious to do so.

"And you think judges are any less afraid of getting trapped in foldspace?" she asked, too tired to be politic anymore.

"I think judges on a starbase have the luxury of not worrying about it," the Old Man said.

Just like they did. She had graduated at the top of her class, fielded offers from a variety of firms, and finally chose the prosecutor's office at

Starbase Sigma because Starbase Sigma was the newest starbase. It would remain operational long after she was dead. She wouldn't have to be moved from one base to another, as the office moved forward with the Fleet.

"They understand the threat," she said.

"They also understand the threat to the hierarchy if we don't punish those who decide to take matters into their own hands just because they're on a difficult mission," the Old Man said.

And in those words, she finally understood what was happening. He had been ordered to take this case. The Old Man didn't take orders from many people, and those who could order him didn't do so often.

"Did you try to say no?" she asked him, deciding not to play any of the lawyerly games anymore.

He glanced at the couch. Arias could see it out of the corner of her eye. The shoes twitched, almost as if their owner was a dog dreaming doggy dreams.

Then the Old Man smiled. It made him look younger, made his silver hair and its unique style look stylish rather than like an older man's vanity. He was almost handsome when he smiled, especially when the smile was real, and not the feral smile he got when he was pursuing a particularly tough case.

"I told them it was a dog of a case," he said. "I said it would hurt the win record of whoever took it."

"And they asked you why you thought you'd lose," she said.

"No," he said. "They told me it was one of the highest profile cases of mutiny to ever occur in the Fleet and if we ignored it we would be inciting anyone trapped in foldspace or on a dangerous mission to stop following protocol. They told me that it would seem like we are condoning the behavior by ignoring it."

"So we should take a case we're going to lose," she said.

"No," he said. "We should take a case that everyone thinks we're going to lose, and then we should prove them wrong."

"*I* should prove them wrong," she said with a sigh.

"Get over yourself, Arias," the Old Man said. "*We* are going to prove them wrong. You are sitting second chair."

She felt a chill run through her. She couldn't remember the last time the Old Man took a case like this.

"You're taking this case?" she asked.

"No," he said. "They're sending in someone special. Danitra Carbone."

One of the best attorneys in the Fleet. A legend. One of the few attorneys who didn't have an office, but who went to the various spots throughout the Fleet and the sectors it crossed to handle important Fleet cases.

Arias had studied Carbone's most famous cases (up to that point) in law school. Arias had once modeled herself on Carbone, until Arias had enough faith in herself that she didn't need to model herself on anyone.

"I'd rather not be second on this, sir," Arias said. She hadn't been out of control of a case in more than a decade.

"Yeah, well, I'd rather not give this to you," the Old Man said. "But again, not my choice. If it makes you feel better, any loss in this case goes on her record, not yours."

"No," Arias said quietly. "It doesn't make me feel better at all."

THREE

Eun Ae Mukasey stared at the information the acting captain of the *Renegat,* Raina Serpell, had sent her. Their conversation had been short; Mukasey did not like interacting with potential clients much. Every client had two things: a personality and a story. Some personalities were stronger than the stories. Some stories were stronger than the personalities.

Cases were won with strong stories, not strong personalities, so Mukasey preferred to see the story first and assess the personality second.

She paced around her small office on Starbase Sigma. The office was on a lower level, away from the shops and the restaurants and the hotels, away from the business sector of the starbase, and closer to the docking rings than most people liked to be.

The courts were sixteen levels up, off in their own wing. Most lawyers had offices near there, and while she thought that convenient, she did not need the convenience.

This case intrigued her. The story was fascinating, and already in the media, at least the media around Starbase Sigma. That could work to her advantage if she took the case. Survivors against all odds, now being prosecuted by the very people they had tried to return to.

They had no real defenders because they had no friends or family left. They had returned one hundred years in their future to find the future more unwelcoming than they had expected.

She could argue that. She wove her way around the five chairs scattered through the small space. This room served as a work area and as an interview room. She had one tiny tiny closet-sized room through an unmarked door where she kept the physical evidence she needed for a case, as well as the anything else proprietary, like tablets and case-sensitive files on a non-networked system. She had several non-networked systems, because she had several cases at the moment.

She would have to jettison a few of them or hand them off to the assistants who floated between her office and three other defense attorneys' offices. She had started that system when she didn't earn enough to pay a junior lawyer or a law clerk; but that system worked so well for her that now that she could afford several junior lawyers on staff, she still didn't hire any.

Everyone still thought she was worth nearly nothing, and she kept it that way. She liked the perception that she lived a hardscrabble life because she had to, not because she wanted to.

And there was really no one to contradict her. She didn't have time for close friends, and she wasn't in any kind of relationship right now.

She scanned the information, looking for more. Serpell had been honest with her in that brief conversation; she said she had already talked to a dozen defense attorneys and they had turned the case down.

Mukasey hadn't asked why the attorneys turned the case down or even who they were. She had a hunch she already knew. Everyone went to the defense attorneys with the spotless records first, not realizing that those records were cherry-picked, along with the cases, to show how great the lawyer was, rather than someone who worked with the client's best interest at heart.

But that thought of the client stopped her for a moment. She studied the faces of the potential clients, which she had on a flat, two-dimensional clear screen. The faces looked like they were some kind of art installation floating against her undecorated far wall.

She often did that to get a sense of people—not just the ones she might represent, but potential witnesses as well.

She usually didn't study the faces. She usually let them scroll, figuring her peripheral vision would tell her much more than any direct-on study would.

These people seemed ordinary. They seemed like people she would have passed in the corridors of the most public section of the starbase, heading to the shops or the restaurants or making it through their daily routines.

They didn't look like hardened criminals, and they certainly didn't look like people who would overthrow their captain, take control of a ship, disgorge much of its crew (or whatever happened to them) and travel back over a long distance and one hundred years just to get arrested.

They didn't look like adventurers either.

They looked unremarkable, even Serpell with her thin brown hair and roundish face. The only one who looked like trouble was Yusef Kabac, who had a thick black scruffy beard and uncut black hair and what seemed to Mukasey to be wild eyes.

If she were running the prosecution's case, she would make Kabac the face of the defendants. She touched the image, and moved it off the scrolling list onto its own little screen. Yeah, he looked like a crazed maniac, one of those messianic types who showed up every generation or two and led the spineless on some kind of half-assed mission that ended up badly for everyone.

Mukasey stuck her hands in the back pocket of the black pants she wore on non-court days, and rocked backwards on her flat shoes.

If she took the case, she would have to isolate crazy-seeming guy or marginalize him or something.

But she still wasn't certain if she would take the case. The prosecution wanted this one to be a big deal. They had brought in Danitra Carbone to head the team. Carbone had a reputation as big as the sector and she deserved it.

Mukasey had never gone head-to-head with her, and Mukasey wanted to. But she couldn't just take the case because she wanted to best the best in the business. She had to take a *good* case to face off with Carbone.

Mukasey had lost a lot, but she had gained a lot from her losses. Not just experience, but a reputation as a fighter, someone who actually cared about her clients and wouldn't leave them in any kind of lurch.

The problem with this case wasn't Carbone or the massive publicity this case would generate. Nor was the problem the story. The story helped a great deal. The problem wasn't even crazy-eyes Kabac.

The problem was that she would be representing 193 people at the same time, all of whom would believe they deserved a bit of her time.

She did not have the resources to handle all of them. She wasn't sure she even wanted to *talk* with all of them. If she took this case, she would have to hire help for the duration, which would be a problem.

The case already looked like a financial loser. Even though these people had salaries in escrow, they couldn't tap the salaries until the case was over. And then, if she lost, (if *they* lost), they'd lose any salary that they would have received on this journey.

Although…she frowned at the faces scrolling on that continual loop. They should have been entitled to other money. Inheritances from family and people left behind.

About twenty years after the *Renegat* disappeared, the crew on that ship should have been declared dead, their assets (if they had any not on a ship) would have been sent to others, and any family wealth would have gone to the wrong heirs.

There might be money here after all.

But she had to test that first.

She selected crazy-eyes Kabac for her first search.

It only took a few minutes to research his family background, because he had none. His parents had died when he was young. He had no siblings, and he had never married.

Which probably explained the look of desperation that was etched on his face.

So Mukasey looked up another face—a woman named Jorja Lakinas who had sustained serious injuries while defending the captain. That information was right at the top of her file, and it made her sympathetic. She had returned to the Fleet, after trying to prevent a mutiny. She should not have been tried for it.

Mukasey made a mental note of that, then looked for Lakinas's family.

She had none either. Parents dead, siblings dead, divorced, no children. No distant cousins either—and all of this had happened *before* Lakinas had joined the *Renegat.*

Mukasey picked four more random faces, found similar stories in all of them. No family. No friends. No one who really missed them.

This was too common among the *Renegat* crew to be a coincidence.

She froze the scrolling faces and tapped her hand against her side.

Why would the Fleet staff a single vessel with crew who had no family to leave behind? Why, in fact, would the Fleet staff a security vessel and send it—*alone*—on a top-secret mission *backwards* and across such a great distance that no Fleet vessel had ever traveled it before?

She sank into one of the chairs, half-smiling at herself.

She was hooked. Not so much on the story of the rescue or anything else that had hit the media around Starbase Sigma.

But hooked on the mystery of the *Renegat* and her crew.

Hooked on the idea that there was a great deal more here than could be found in a simple search, a great deal more than she had expected when she spoke to Serpell.

Mukasey cursed good-naturedly. This case was going to cost her in both time and money.

But it would do something more for her. It would keep her interested, keep her sharp, and keep her thinking.

She needed that. Every now and then, a woman needed both a mission and a mystery to keep her going.

Looked like she had found both.

FOUR

Danitra Carbone sat in the gigantic suite at the back of her private runabout. She had information sprawled across the three bolted-in couches, two tables, and four chairs. All of them doubled as screens, and usually she liked that, walking from bits of furniture to other bits of furniture to get her information.

But on this day, she felt overwhelmed by all of it.

Not to mention the fact that she was furious.

She hadn't been assigned a case in nearly a decade. She had been *offered* cases, told that they might benefit her, or that they might improve her already spectacular career. Sometimes she would be nudged—hard—by her superiors. Sometimes she would be discouraged just as hard by those same superiors.

But they always let her choose. And she usually ignored the nudging, believing that she knew what she could handle better than anyone else.

This time, though, she hadn't been nudged. She'd been shoved onto this case, told she couldn't refuse it. She had actually asked what would happen if she did, and the response was swift:

You know what happens to a Fleet officer who disobeys a direct order.

Sometimes she forgot she was an officer in the Fleet. She had acted without supervision for so long that she felt like an independent contractor, just like the attorneys she often faced in court.

She had never envied them before, thinking of them instead with just a bit of pity, since they had to not only compete for cases, they also had to fund their own offices. They had to assemble their own resources when she had all of the resources in the Fleet at her fingertips.

Normally, she would have turned this case down. It looked like one of the worst cases she had ever been offered, because it was a loser no matter what happened.

If she lost, well, then she would have that on her quite spectacular record.

But if she won, she would still lose, because she would be responsible for imprisoning two hundred people who had apparently wanted nothing more than to return home to their friends and family. And who could blame them, really? It sounded like they had all gone through hell to get back to the Fleet, and then the Fleet was going to punish them for being successful.

Her greatest frustration, after two days of digging into this damn thing, was that she couldn't find a middle ground. She needed to either vilify these people or somehow make the Fleet's needs paramount to the survivors' and she wasn't sure how to do either.

There had to be another way out of this bind, but even after looking, she couldn't find it.

It wouldn't matter if the court gagged the proceedings. All that meant was that the media in this sector would not cover the case detail-by-detail. The results, no matter what they were, would become big news.

And she would be vilified for prosecuting these people or she would be ridiculed for losing something that seemed so easy. Or both.

Of course, she was probably already being vilified. She wasn't yet at Starbase Sigma, but she would be arriving soon.

Then she would get to meet the locals on her team. They had been chosen for her as well, something that also irritated her. She normally would get to choose who would sit beside her on a case this important, but of course, she wasn't even getting that courtesy.

Although she didn't want to complain too loudly, because she would have probably chosen Lucinda Arias no matter what. Arias was good, and some day might be spectacular.

Maybe someone in the Fleet wanted Carbone to train Arias. But hidden in that idea was the thought that Carbone was past her prime, when she felt like she had just hit it.

She sighed and hoped that the locals would have provided a space for her inside of the prosecutor's office. She needed a place to settle in, one that would allow her to run her war boards and her mock trials and maybe even depose all of the witnesses she needed.

She ran a hand through her hair, trying to beat the frustration back. She couldn't go into this case angry. Nor could she go into it thinking she would lose.

She had to go into it like she went into every other case in her career. She had to go into it to win.

And not just win.

In this one, she needed to convince everyone—not just the court—that these people were guilty of the highest crime in the Fleet. They were guilty of attempting to murder the leader of their small universe.

They were guilty of upending the Fleet itself.

FIVE

They gave Danitra Carbone the biggest private office in the prosecutor's wing. Arias had been coveting that office. Hell, she'd been coveting any office. She still sat in the bullpen with all of the other prosecutors.

Before Carbone arrived, though, the Old Man asked Arias to set up Carbone's office, which gave Arias a chance to wander through it. And as she did, she discovered the smaller private office through a set of double doors.

She supposed that smaller office was for personal use for the Great Being who worked in the larger room. But she didn't care. She moved all of her stuff to that private office, figuring she was going to be Carbone's second, so she was going to be as close to Carbone as she possibly could.

The Old Man caught Arias moving her stuff about an hour in. He watched, then followed her into the private office. She braced herself for a massive tongue-lashing.

Instead, he pushed a small button on the wall opposite the larger office, and a single door formed on the outside wall of the small office. That door opened into the corridor. Now the office that Arias stole looked more like a personal office rather than the private room it had been designed as.

She had given him a grateful look. He had grinned, that look that made him look young and impish, and made her wonder again what he had been like back in the day.

He didn't say a word otherwise. He left after a few minutes, and she didn't even see him go.

Arias settled into the new office, working as if it were her own. Over the next day or so, she did make it her own. She loved the privacy, the lack of conversation, that smell of sweat and nerves that always came with anyone entering the bullpen.

Her job actually felt like something she could grasp and hold rather than a fighter ship she was grabbing onto as it flew out on a mission.

It got easier because Carbone hadn't shown up as expected. Oh, she was on the starbase, but after her runabout docked, she didn't come to the office. She hadn't shown up the next morning either, and for a while, Arias assumed (hoped) that she would have both offices to herself.

Then she came back after a late dinner, only to find all of the lights blazing in the inside office. She wandered in, and saw the great woman in the flesh, both smaller and wider than Arias had expected, as if Carbone's skin couldn't quite contain the force of her personality.

Carbone didn't hear Arias arrive, or at least, Carbone hadn't acknowledged her arrival. Carbone had brought in half a dozen tablets, black with silver trim, which made them much sleeker than anything Arias had seen on the starbase. Carbone had her graying hair piled on top of her head, held there with some kind of comb. The hair's tight curls, which had always exploded outward in the holos Arias had seen of Carbone's court appearances, seemed like they were going to burst out of the combs at any moment.

In fact, everything about Carbone looked like contained energy. She moved slowly, but as if she were holding back, as if moving fast would somehow ruin everything she was trying to do.

"I'm assuming you're Lucinda Arias," Carbone said, still looking down at her desk. "And if you're going to work with me, then work with me. Don't stare and don't wait for me to tell you what to do."

Arias swallowed hard, annoyed at herself. She was a full professional, someone who had done this job for decades, and she was good at it.

Yet she still felt like a beginner as she stood there, like someone who needed full instruction on everything she had ever done.

"I *am* Lucinda Arias," she said, glad her voice remained under her control. She crossed the room, extending her hand. "I'm pleased to meet you."

"Yeah, yeah," Carbone said. "I don't do handshakes. They're a cultural relic. I don't do formal introductions either. You know who I am, I know who you are, we've already formed opinions on each other, and now that we're going to work together, we'll see if those opinions are right or wrong. So, let's get started."

Arias couldn't tell if the speech was planned and designed to intimidate her, or if that was just an unintended consequence of Carbone's focus.

Arias stopped in front of the desk, saw even more tablets, wondered if they were all for this case.

"Look," she said. "I know you were assigned me as a second, and I know you need someone local to help with the customs here, but if you want someone else—"

"I would have asked." Carbone lifted her head. "I don't want to be here any more than you do. Your boss already told me you think this case is a loser. And, on its face, it's not going to help either one of us. To ease your mind, I would have chosen you as my local no matter what. I don't compliment people to make them feel better, so you can trust what I said here. Okay? Now, let's get to work. I assume you've already investigated some approaches here…?"

"I have," Arias said. "We have a surprising amount of information about the mutiny, given the fact that the *Renegat* blew up a few hours after it arrived near the *Aiszargs*."

"Yeah, yeah," Carbone said. "The *Aiszargs* was extremely efficient, which actually works against us. Half the people we're prosecuting were nowhere near the captain when he was murdered."

So she had already looked at the data. Arias let out a small breath of relief and hoped Carbone hadn't seen it. Arias had been afraid that Carbone would slough off all of the hard work on her.

Nice to see that wasn't what was going to happen.

"Worse," Arias said, "at least six of them, maybe more, fought at the captain's side that day."

"Saw that." Carbone fell into her chair as if her legs had given out.

She actually let out a small *woof* as if sitting had knocked some of the wind out of her. "I'm thinking of separating them out, maybe giving them a plea or having them testify against the others."

"We can't separate them out," Arias said. "We have strict orders to treat them all as a single entity."

Carbone's dark eyes flashed, and her lips turned up slightly. "I looked at your record," she said. "I would never have thought you would be the kind of person who would let someone else dictate your case."

"I'm a prosecutor," Arias said. "I don't always get to pick."

Carbone turned her head, as if Arias's words hit her harder than expected.

Then she nodded, as if she had just had a private conversation with herself.

"Our case," she said. "We get to build it. And those six are going to force us to lose. We take control of that. We don't ask the court's permission. We just do."

Arias had done that a few times, but never on a case as important or visible as this one. Usually on cases she didn't want to bring to trial, especially a trial before panel of judges.

"You don't like that idea," Carbone said.

"I haven't thought about it enough to have an opinion," Arias said.

"Don't lie to me, girl," Carbone said. "You don't like it."

Great. Carbone could read her, and only after a few minutes. Very few people could read Arias that well, and usually that happened after months, maybe years.

"I was thinking of a different tactic," Arias said. "Everyone on that ship knew that Nadim Crowe and his engineers were unhappy, and their unhappiness provoked the crisis. *Everyone.* And no one did anything about it. I was thinking of arguing that the six should have acted sooner, and it was their guilty consciences that made them stand beside Preemas, not because they believed in him, but because they were afraid they'd be blamed for the actions of Crowe and his friends."

"Convoluted," Carbone said. "Convoluted is hard to argue."

"Maybe," Arias said. "But the whole case is convoluted. All these people wanted was to come home. The *Renegat* was a last-chance career builder for them, in theory anyway, a way of recouping all the screwups in their careers. We show what they did as another screwup. Especially since everyone on that ship had an escape route built in."

Carbone raised her head, eyes hooded. She seemed intrigued. Arias wished she could read Carbone as well as Carbone already read her.

"Preemas made an unscheduled stop at Sector Base Z. He let anyone who wanted to leave the ship for good, and he brought in new crew members while there," Arias said.

"Yeah," Carbone said. "If they didn't like how he was running the ship or the mission, they could have left. Seems their defense will argue that."

Arias shook her head. "There was no career path for anyone who got off on Sector Base Z. They were officially done."

"Maybe that's what happened, but they couldn't have known that."

"Oh, but they did," Arias said. "The leader, this Raina Serpell, she nearly stayed at Sector Base Z. But she knew her career would be over. She talked to a number of people about it, especially after her wife died."

"Her wife fought at Preemas's side," Carbone said.

"Stupidly," Arias said. "And got even more people killed."

Carbone stared at her. "Your argument is confusing me."

"This was a ship headed for disaster," Arias said. "Preemas knew it. There was unrest from the start, but none of these people left. They all knew something bad was going to happen. They stayed."

"Thin," Carbone said. "We need the six."

"If we separate them," Arias said, feeling some frustration, "then the court's wish that these people be seen as one unit gets broken. They'll be individuals, and we'll spend days arguing 193 different cases."

Carbone moved some of the tablets aside. She appeared to be thinking.

"If I were stuck with this case by myself," Arias said, "I would argue that these 193 people were opposed to being led by Nadim Crowe, not that they were supporting Preemas. I would argue that they were complicit in his death, because that was the only way they would get any credit when they returned to the Fleet."

Carbone frowned at her.

"They thought they were returning to their time," Arias said. "They were supposed to bring back information about that Scrapheap. Relevant information to the Fleet of one hundred years ago, not irrelevant information to the Fleet we know now. They might have been hailed as heroes. They could blame Crowe for Preemas's death, something they really did not try to prevent, most of them, and then they could claim success on the mission itself."

Carbone made a *humph* sound. She clearly hadn't thought of any of that.

Then she nodded. "You're right. We can't look at this in the context of the Fleet now. We have to look at it in the context of the Fleet then."

Arias tried not to smile in triumph.

"I'm not sure if I agree with your argument," Carbone said. "But it gives us a place to start. You research the Fleet. Let's figure out if we were different people one hundred years ago."

That sounded like dismissive make-work. Arias's triumph fled.

"And what will you do?" she asked.

"Interview the six, of course," Carbone said. "If we can kill this case in its crib, I want to do so, and I want to do so now."

SIX

Before Mukasey conducted any interviews with her new clients, before she looked at the résumés of the additional help that she would need to run this case, before she even tried to build the case, she researched the judges.

The panel was set. The timeline was in place, which sometimes happened with big cases. The Fleet didn't like deep dives into cases. The Fleet didn't like cases to run for months, let alone years, as a case like this could have.

So the judges were assigned, the calendars were in place, and the lawyers knew what points they had to hit when.

Twelve judges, all of whom coordinated their schedules with each other before anyone had even contacted Danitra Carbone.

But as Mukasey started to research them, she found something interesting. Three judges had recused themselves from this case.

One had a family emergency that took her to Sector Base A-2. She couldn't guarantee that she would be able to sit on the case at all.

The other wanted to retire as a judge. Apparently, he didn't like the workload, and this case would have guaranteed months of hard work for him, something he loathed.

The third gave no reason at all for her recusal except a conflict of interest.

Conflict of interest. On a ship that had emerged from foldspace one hundred years after it had entered.

Mukasey was intrigued. She had won cases before by investigating bits and pieces outside the usual scope of the case.

This was something she might be able to use.

She placed it at the top of the pile to investigate, and because it involved a long-time judge, she would do the investigation herself.

SEVEN

Someone had repaired Jorja Lakinas poorly. If Carbone had been a different kind of attorney, she would have gone after the medical professional who left Lakinas in this state.

Instead, Carbone sat across from Lakinas in a private meeting room in the tower that housed the survivors of the *Renegat*. The tower had been built on the starbase's eleventh level and looked like it had been grafted onto the walls accidentally. The tower was tall and narrow and had no windows overlooking the rest of the level—at least that Carbone could see.

She had come in a side door, and taken a private elevator down two floors. She had to use a code to do so. Apparently, Lakinas did not want anyone to know she was meeting with one of the prosecutors, and Carbone couldn't blame her.

Carbone couldn't even request that Lakinas come to the prosecutor's offices, because that would take court involvement, and a special order. The *Renegat* survivors weren't supposed to leave this small section of the starbase.

Carbone hadn't told Arias or anyone else in the office that she was coming. Arias didn't approve of separating out the six, but Carbone felt she had to try. The six who had fought with Preemas would tank her case if just one judge thought that detail important.

Besides, Carbone was a bit leery of the attorney the survivors had hired. Unlike most defendants facing a case like this, the survivors had not chosen an attorney with a perfect win record. Instead, the attorney's record balanced wins and losses, which meant she actually thought about her cases.

Carbone was going to have to study this attorney's methods, because the win/loss ratio suggested an occasionally outside-of-the-box approach to defense. Which meant that Carbone would not be able to run the court the way she usually did.

At the moment, though, Carbone was studying Lakinas. The poor woman had been shot several times in the battle on the *Renegat*. She had gotten terrible medical care on the *Renegat* itself, and by the time she had gotten back to the Fleet, her wounds had healed improperly. The Fleet let her get some surgery to repair the wounds that threatened her life, but they had done little else.

Carbone was going to argue for the cosmetic work—if she couldn't persuade Lakinas and the other five to turn on their friends. The last thing Carbone wanted was for the judges to see this face. This face might make them sympathetic to the defense's cause.

At first glance, the face looked like any other. Then the light would catch it, and the skin would seem too stretched over the cheekbones, too shiny. Lakinas's eyes were recessed into that face, making her look gravely ill. Under her hairline, a white scar was visible, the kind of scar that usually only showed up when someone was in the middle of procedures, not when procedures were over.

The edges of Lakinas's mouth were uneven and her nose looked crooked. Taken together, the parts worked at a distance, but up close Lakinas looked like a ship that had been built out of mismatched parts.

Lakinas had been sitting in a chair when Carbone arrived. Lakinas had pushed a table aside so that Carbone could see Lakinas's entire body. Her feet were twisted inward, her left hand was clawed nearly shut, and her torso hunched forward. She couldn't have been comfortable in the chair she sat in, but Carbone wasn't sure if Lakinas could stand for long periods of time.

A cart that could carry Lakinas from place to place leaned against the wall, but Carbone wasn't sure if that was for emergencies or if Lakinas actually used it all the time.

As Carbone entered, Lakinas watched her. Carbone could see the defiance in that face.

Carbone met Lakinas's gaze head on, then deliberately looked Lakinas up and down, assessing her. Carbone had met seriously injured people before, albeit usually before they had been repaired, and they were used to others looking away.

Carbone had learned there was a lot of power in looking at the injured directly.

"I'm not supposed to be meeting with you," Lakinas said after a minute.

Carbone made a mental note of that: Lakinas was impatient. She didn't try to stare back at Carbone and make this some kind of competition. She needed to get the meeting underway.

"I asked you to bring your attorney," Carbone said.

"I don't have an attorney who is just mine," Lakinas said. "I have the group attorney and I didn't think it was wise to bring her."

So Lakinas was a bit more canny than Carbone had given her credit for.

"I understand you fought side by side with Captain Preemas in the Battle for the *Renegat,*" Carbone said.

"Is that what they're calling it now?" Lakinas said. "The battle for the *Renegat*?"

Carbone had made that up herself, but she wasn't going to admit that. "Some are, yes," she said.

"I fought with him," Lakinas said.

"Is that where you got the injuries?" Carbone said.

"Some of them," Lakinas said.

Carbone hadn't expected that response. "Some of them?"

"They put me in the brig, injured," she said. "I tried get out."

"They?" Carbone asked.

"Crowe's people." Lakinas's lips turned downward. "They won, you know."

Carbone nodded. She knew the outlines of all of this, but the actual details were not at her fingertips yet. She knew that Crowe and his people had sent some of the people who had fought with Preemas to the med bay and the rest to the brig, but she hadn't realized that some of the injured went to the brig too.

"Did they know you were injured?" Carbone asked.

Lakinas let out a bitter laugh. "Kinda hard to miss."

"And they didn't offer you medical attention?" Carbone asked.

"Nope," Lakinas said. Then she shifted in her chair. The movement looked painful, and it took all of Carbone's control to prevent a wince.

But apparently that didn't work, because Lakinas gave her a withering look, a kind of *don't pity me, don't think you understand me* look. Carbone silently cursed herself.

She didn't want to be that readable, but it was hard, particularly with someone as damaged as Lakinas. Lakinas didn't easily fit into the kinds of categories that Carbone was used to putting people into, so Lakinas had an advantage.

Carbone hated it when someone else had an advantage.

"Look," Lakinas said, "you want to question me, you do it formally. This is some kind of sideways crap, isn't it? You want something from me."

Carbone had to give it to her: Lakinas was bright and canny and shouldn't be underestimated.

"I'd like to make you an offer," Carbone said. "We handle your medical care, get you as fixed up as possible, give you some reparations for your time and effort on the *Renegat*, and remove all of the mutiny charges."

"In exchange for what?" Lakinas said.

"Testimony if we need it," Carbone said. "Testimony about the other defendants."

"You think I have something nasty to say about them?" Lakinas asked.

"Do you?" Carbone asked.

Lakinas let out a small snort. "As people? Yeah, I do. As mutineers—as you're calling them—no. They're just ignorant idiots who did their best to return here."

Carbone felt a bit of shock at Lakinas's bitterness. "And you? Why did you come back?"

"You think I would have joined up with the people who tried to kill me?" she asked. "What are you, nuts? And why are you going after everyone anyway? They didn't do anything."

Carbone suppressed a sigh. She wasn't sure if Lakinas was still playing her. If she was, it was a smart move. Because Lakinas could get everything Carbone offered, and not testify. Lakinas would get her life back for simply removing herself from the case.

Maybe Lakinas didn't need an attorney. Maybe she was smart enough to handle all of this on her own.

That too wasn't something Carbone was used to.

"The offer lasts for the duration of this conversation," Carbone said.

"I haven't got anything bad to say about the others on the *Renegat*," Lakinas said. "The ones who brought me back here. I got nothing bad to say."

Carbone almost said, *I don't want bad*, but she did. She needed it.

"I understand," she said. "You can provide context though."

"You have me testify," Lakinas said, "and I'll defend everyone you're trying to prosecute. They kept me alive."

"I understand," Carbone repeated. She wouldn't make Lakinas testify—at least, not in front of the judges. But she might see if she could manipulate a deposition, and get part of it admitted into the record. If the defense attorney did not get a chance to ask Lakinas how she felt about the others, or if Carbone could manage that response, keep it from the judges, then she would be able to use things Lakinas told her.

"You want something else," Lakinas said.

Initially, Carbone had. She had wanted Lakinas to talk to the other five who had fought alongside Preemas. But now Carbone didn't want her to. Carbone wanted to know if any of them had information she could use against the remaining defendants. She would do the interviews herself.

"I want an answer," Carbone said. "Because this initial conversation is nearly over."

Lakinas's broken mouth twisted into a bitter smile. "You want me to betray the people who got me home, maybe even saved my life. If I leave

—if those of us who fought at the captain's side—leave this case, then you have a shot of winning it, don't you?"

Carbone's heartbeat increased. This woman somehow understood how the law worked. That surprised Carbone. She wasn't used to dealing with someone on the other side of the table who understood what she was doing.

"The offer," Carbone said. "Your time is running out."

"It's a good offer for me," Lakinas said. "If I take it, I prove to myself that I'm the asshole I think I am."

The self-loathing nearly took Carbone's breath away.

"You got five others to talk with," Lakinas said. "They all have to leave for you to be successful."

Carbone did not move. It was fascinating to listen to this woman consider her options in real time.

"You came to me first. I'm the most injured, the easiest mark. You thought you could get me to talk to them, right? And now you're not asking me because you understand that I won't." Lakinas shifted in her chair again, that flicker of pain crossing her face one more time.

Carbone did not move. She didn't dare. This was her best chance of winning the case, and she wasn't going to let it go easily. But she knew better than to try to persuade Lakinas. Lakinas was the kind of woman who would strengthen under pressure, not bow to it.

"Money, possible repair, a life." Lakinas nodded. "You have a lot riding on this to offer so much without asking for anything in return."

She hit it in one. She knew exactly what she was talking about.

"So I have to figure out what my own interests are," Lakinas said. "Can I continue living like this to stick it to you and people like you? The ones who care about winning more than they care about what's right?"

Her mouth twisted even more.

"And worse," she said, "if I say no and the others say yes, you're never going to offer this to me again."

It was her only miss. Carbone would have to offer it again, because Lakinas could sink the case all by herself.

"What would I have to do?" Lakinas asked. "Agree to never testify? Refuse to talk to the defense? Not give my story?"

All of the above, Carbone thought, but did not say.

"You're not going to answer that, are you?" Lakinas asked. "Because if you did, then you would tip your hand even more."

Lakinas let out a sigh, then brought up her cramped hand and stared at it, as if she had never seen it before.

Then she let her hand drop back to her lap.

"The ironic thing is," she said, "I can't live with either choice. I betray everything I believe in to get my health back or I remain like this, at least until the *Renegat* Renegades win their case. If they win their case."

She shook her head, then winced. Carbone tried to ignore the woman's obvious pain, but it wasn't working. It was almost impossible to ignore.

"I fought at Preemas's side because it was the right thing to do even though he was an egotistical idiot who was probably going to get us killed. *All* of us fought at his side because it was the right thing to do. All six of us, the ones you want to turn."

Lakinas's gaze met Carbone's.

"We put the Fleet above our own self-interest. And now the Fleet is screwing with us." Lakinas raised her chin slightly. The movement put an obvious strain on the muscles in her neck. "You know what, Danitra Carbone? You're a lawyer. You're supposed to respect the rules. Yet here you are, meeting with me against most of the rules, trying to make a side deal that will benefit you. You care about the win, not about what's right."

And that sentence made Carbone's heart sink.

"You found a bunch of believers," Lakinas said. "We know that the system is screwed up, but it's what we've got, and we fought nearly to the death to defend it. You're a representative of that system. You should have fought too. You should have told your idiot superiors that this case wasn't worth taking. You shouldn't have put your name on it."

Carbone almost—almost—opened her mouth to defend herself. She caught herself just in time.

But Lakinas seemed to notice. "Yeah, they ordered you to take it. They're making it hard for you. But you're that person who needs an even greater challenge each and every time to tackle something. And this is a big challenge, isn't it?"

Carbone did not answer. Lakinas was right, but she didn't need the verbal confirmation.

"So..." Lakinas said, that broken mouth forming a full smile. The full smile made her face seem even more mismatched. "I'm going to make it harder for you. You're the representative of everything I dislike about the Fleet. I'm a true believer in all we do, in the rules and the regulations and the systems we've set up from the beginning. And I hate people like you who circumvent it."

Hate. That was a word Carbone could hang onto. She'd been hated by people on the other side before. She didn't mind being hated.

"I'm going to say no to your generous self-serving offer. And even if my five colleagues say yes, you're still screwed. Because I will testify, and I will show those judges that we were fighting *for* the Fleet, not against it."

Lakinas put her good hand on the table.

"And when this is all over," she said, "and you've lost, I'm going to make sure that the Fleet does all the things you offered. They're going to repair me, they're going to give me a good place to live, and they're going to take care of me."

Carbone sat perfectly still.

Lakinas's hand wobbled, then that wobble went up her arm. Carbone realized too late that Lakinas was trying to stand.

Something must have crossed Carbone's face, because Lakinas gave her a warning look.

"In fact," Lakinas said as she struggled to her feet. "You've inspired me. I will hire my own attorney. To get what I need now. How will that sit with your judges? To know that I'm fighting to get the medical care I've deserved all along?"

She clawed at the cart and it floated over to her, lowering to chair height.

She sat on the edge of it and stared at Carbone. Lakinas's eyes glittered with so much anger that Carbone sat back in her seat.

"Thank you," Lakinas said. "I had lost focus since we returned. I was staring at a life filled with painful medical procedures and a lot of misunderstanding. A life that wasn't about me, not really. A life outside my control."

She laughed. The sound chilled Carbone all the way to her soul.

"I have a focus now, Danitra," Lakinas said, not even trying to be respectful. "I'm going to make sure you lose the biggest case of your life. Consider yourself notified. And if you screw with me, I'll screw with you right back."

Somehow the cart helped her swing her legs onto it. Then she drove it out of the room, the door opening as the cart reached it.

Carbone sat at the table for a long, long moment, staring at the slowly closing door.

She had been threatened by defendants and witnesses before. She'd faced hatred before.

But she had never misread a case like this one.

Arias hadn't wanted to talk to the six. Arias had a finger on the pulse of this case. And Carbone didn't know how.

She wondered if it was too late to back out.

And what would hurt her reputation more. Leaving the case now, or losing it.

Because she didn't think she had any other options.

Not anymore.

EIGHT

The Old Man didn't have an office, so Arias had to chase him all over the building. Old Man sightings seemed more like vague promises than reality after a half an hour. Either that, or he was avoiding her.

Probably avoiding her, since he had to know how furious she was.

The biggest screwup of her career, and she didn't do it. She had argued against it. But she was second on this case, without control of it, and she had no rights here. So she was going to change that.

She finally returned to her desk in the bullpen to find the Old Man leaning against it, arms crossed, looking vaguely amused. His legs were crossed at the ankles, one knee bent, so that he seemed relaxed. Maybe he was.

"You were looking for me?" he asked.

"Don't play games with me," she snapped. "I need to talk to you and you know why."

"So talk," he said.

She looked around the bullpen. The nearest lawyer was five desks back, struggling to pick up a stack of tablets and some files.

"Not in public," she said.

"This isn't public," he said.

"Well," she said, "we can't go to the office I stole."

The one near Danitra Carbone's office. Arias didn't trust Carbone to let them talk in private.

"Give us the room," the Old Man shouted.

Three lawyers sat up on couches. Arias hadn't even seen them. One, a young man she didn't recognize, had to be new. His hair stuck up in tufts. He'd clearly been sleeping.

The other two were used to being yelled at by the Old Man. They rolled off their couches, grabbed a bag with their stuff and stumbled out. The woman who'd been fighting with her tablets took one off the top and glared at all of them before stomping off.

The need for privacy was probably interfering with her work on a case.

Arias waited until the room was empty, then said, "You know what she did."

Arias didn't even have to use Carbone's name. The Old Man would know what Arias was talking about.

"Talked to a defendant without the defendant's lawyer present. For the record, the defendant waived her right—"

"I don't care," Arias said. "She tried to separate the defendant from the group. The court ordered that the group *be* a group. And she ignored the court's order, trying to bargain separately. The court has noticed, and—"

"And you got your hand slapped," the Old Man said. "You've experienced worse."

Arias's eyes narrowed. "She pissed off the defendant, and she gave the other side notice that we're afraid of the fact that six of those defendants can demonstrably prove that they fought at Preemas's side."

The Old Man's gaze was flat.

"We've lost the case before we even go in," Arias said.

"And you want me to, what, exactly?" he asked, all trace of amusement gone.

"Vacate the case," she said. "Refuse to play anymore. Let those poor people alone."

"Because you're going to lose?" his voice held a trace of sarcasm. "Or because you're going to lose due to someone else's mistake?"

Her face warmed, but not because he shamed her. He infuriated her.

"Prosecuting them is wrong. So let's just stop here," she said.

He nodded. "We're under orders."

"I. Don't. Care," she said.

He pushed off her desk. "If I get rid of Carbone, can you win this?"

"No," she said. "Not without getting rid of those six people."

He nodded, then studied her. "I never heard you admit defeat before you even start."

"I've started," Arias said. "I'm deep into this case. The evidence is a mess, the situation is strange, and these people struggled to rejoin the Fleet after foldspace issues, so they are sympathetic."

"Have you ever asked why?" he asked.

"Why what?" she asked.

"Why they struggled to come back. Wouldn't it have been wiser to remain near that Scrapheap? The *Renegat* wasn't functioning properly back there, and none of them—not a single one—had real engineering experience."

"Kabac did," she muttered.

"And he was fired from his engineering positions."

She lifted her head, seeing the Old Man clearly for the first time this day. He had been studying the evidence. He knew this case.

He knew how to prosecute it.

"What's your theory of the case?" she asked.

He clearly noted her different tone. He smiled.

"I'm so glad you asked," he said.

NINE

Mukasey did not trust good news. Not when she was working on a case. The fact that Danitra Carbone had talked to Jorja Lakinas and had essentially bribed her to leave the case—without an attorney present—was a gift, especially since Lakinas had refused.

But it wasn't the kind of gift that Mukasey wanted. She had already planned on using the six Preemas defenders in her argument. She would have used them even if they accepted Carbone's bribe and left the group in the first place.

The case suddenly felt like a winner and that bothered her. She'd lost more sure-winners than any other kind of case.

So she was working sixteen-hour days and dreaming about the case at night. She had assistants. She had them going through the footage she'd managed to get through discovery, footage of the security feeds on the *Renegat*. She had them work the day-to-day, starting with the communications back to the Fleet.

The assistants had found a lot more than she expected. The communications had been scrubbed, and not recently. Not even after the *Renegat* left the Scrapheap.

Before.

Well before.

Mukasey had been working the battle itself, trying to figure out who was where, before she launched the client interviews. They were going to be a lot of work, and she wasn't looking forward to it. She didn't dare miss a single client, either, because the one she missed might be the one with the most important story, the one with the telling detail.

And she'd been trying to track down the judge who recused herself. The judge was a former admiral—and this judge had once been in charge of Scrapheaps for the Fleet. And her name did appear in the file for the *Renegat*.

She had been a vice-admiral at the time, and she had been the one who put together the initial mission.

Her name was Bella Gão.

She was older than the stars themselves.

And she probably had a lot of secrets to tell, if only she would be willing to talk.

TEN

The Old Man put his hands on Arias's desk. He was leaning again, but he didn't have his arms crossed. His entire body was open, relaxed, as if he had been waiting for someone to ask him what he thought of the entire case.

Maybe he had been. Although Arias didn't know why. He could have told her from the start.

"The *Renegat* was a rogue ship," he said.

She frowned at him. She had no idea what he meant.

"The moment that Captain Preemas stopped following the orders he had received, the entire crew should have reported him," the Old Man said. "They had many opportunities. They could have said something at Sector Base Z, which was an unauthorized stop. A few of the crew who had left the ship had done so, but it had proven too late. No one spoke up, at least that I could see from the record. And Preemas headed to the Scrapheap anyway. No one tried to stop him."

The Old Man seemed proud of himself, but Arias couldn't tell why.

"I'm not sure how that matters," she said.

The Old Man gave her a pitying look. "Have you examined the rescue interviews? They're uniform. Nadim Crowe and his people offered everyone on the *Renegat* the chance to stay in that faraway sector, near the Scrapheap, the opportunity to join him in building a new Fleet."

"And the people who came back did not want to join," she said. She hadn't really gone over all of the interviews yet, but she would. She had been a bit busy.

"How do we know?" the Old Man said. "We only have their word. How do we know that they're not here to infiltrate the Fleet itself, overthrow the leadership, and make it easy for Crowe's newly repaired ships to return to us from foldspace?"

She felt a little cold. It sounded weirdly convincing, even though it wasn't at all logical.

"Because they didn't try it," Arias said. "And because they told us what Crowe had intended to do, why he left the *Renegat* in the first place."

"The first rule of deception," the Old Man said. "Tell as much of the truth as possible."

Her frown deepened. She knew that. She'd prosecuted a lot of cases.

"But they didn't try to infiltrate the Fleet," she said.

"They couldn't," the Old Man said. "They lost one hundred years. You've been looking at the history of the Fleet. You've been trying to put this return into that context."

He had been monitoring everything. She was stunned by that.

"You know that they would have been heroes if they had returned then," he said. "They had some information about that Scrapheap that the admirals wanted. They had theories and they had worked their asses off to return. They were ready to be rehabilitated. They would have fought for it."

"That doesn't mean they would have risen in the ranks," Arias said.

"Doesn't it?" he asked.

She stared at him. She honestly didn't know the answer to that. She doubted anyone did. Not many people from that period were still alive, despite the advances in technology that lengthened human life. Humans still lived lives that shortened their existences. Just because living nearly 200 years was possible didn't mean that most people did so.

"All we have to do is argue it," the Old Man said. "We don't have to prove it."

The frown left her face. She could feel it. The tension was gone from her forehead.

"You want to fight this case, don't you?" she asked. "You want to be part of it."

"I'm fascinated by it," he said.

She had never heard the Old Man say that.

"And," he added, "it's the only way to get rid of Carbone."

He was right. Just because Carbone had screwed up didn't mean the Fleet would remove her from the case. But if they replaced her with the Old Man, who was legendary in his approach to cases, and his unwillingness to take on anything but the most challenging work, they might consider letting her go.

"You've already talked to her," Arias said. "She won't step down."

He grinned, then he shrugged, as if to say that what he had done wouldn't matter.

"Well, I didn't tell her my intention," he said. "Because if I take the case—"

"She becomes second," Arias said, unable to repress her own grin.

"Technically," he said, "I would get to choose my second. I would choose you. She would be third."

The assistant, essentially. Running the research, getting coffee, being told where to sit, where to stand, and how to behave.

Arias would bet that Carbone hadn't been in that position in decades.

Arias couldn't stop her grin from growing. She finally felt a bit of hope on this case.

"You're going to send her home," she said.

"Unless you want a high-profile loss on your record," he said. "She could stay. The loss would be the ugliest this office has experienced in decades."

"You're going to tell her that too," Arias said.

"Naw," he said quietly. "After she goes, I'm going to mention it to the media. That boneheaded woman is all reputation and bluster. We need actual lawyers on the case. And we have you."

Arias's breath caught. He had never said anything like that to her before.

"Thank you, sir," she said.

"Never thank me for telling the truth," he said. "It makes truth-telling unusual. I just tell it like I see it."

Then he rapped his hand on the desk, and stood up.

"Let's get the others back in here," he said. "We lost days to Carbone's stupidity. If we're going to win this case, we need to get to work."

Arias smiled. It had been a long time since she worked with the Old Man. But she had done so many times as a young lawyer, and she knew how he operated. He wouldn't try to hog the limelight. He wouldn't take credit for something he did not do.

And, most importantly, he wouldn't make a major decision behind her back. He would consult with her.

They would work as a team.

"Lucinda?" he said, catching her attention. Apparently she hadn't heard his last question. "You do realize that this is pro forma, right?"

This. He wasn't being clear.

"What is, sir?" she asked.

"My heading this prosecution," he said. "You'll head it. After the mess with Carbone settles down."

Arias's smile faded. "Are you sure, sir?" she asked. The last thing she wanted was to think this case was hers only to lose it to him.

"Absolutely," he said. "I don't have time to head a major prosecution like this one and run this office. If anything, I'll be second. I'll keep up on the details, and advise, but you'll lead."

She felt a heady moment of joy, and tamped it down before it interfered with her concentration.

"Thank you, sir," she said.

He waved a hand at her dismissively. "That's how it should have been in the first place," he said. "Glad we can finally make it right."

Then he rapped the desk one last time, stood, and grinned at her.

"We're going to win this one, Arias," he said as he walked away. "I can feel it."

The joy she had felt a moment earlier dissipated. She wished he hadn't said that. Not because she was superstitious—she wasn't. Because she didn't want the expectation.

Then she sighed. She couldn't control how he felt about the case. She could only control how she dealt with the case.

It still felt like a dog of a case to her. She doubted she would win.

But with the Old Man's confidence—and with the fact that she had somehow bested Danitra Carbone without even really trying—Arias at least had a leg up.

She would do everything she could to win—and everything she could was one whole heck of a lot.

ELEVEN

Dismissed.

Danitra Carbone sat in the office they had assigned her on this backwater starbase and stared at the pile of tablets in front of her. She had been given twelve hours to vacate the office, and even then, someone would doublecheck everything she had done to make certain she didn't walk off with evidence or files or equipment she wasn't entitled to.

Dismissed.

She had never been dismissed from a case before. Not in her entire history as a lawyer. Not even as an associate. Not even when she was interning.

No judge had ever taken her off a case, no one had ever requested that she leave.

She had always, always finished what she started—even if she hadn't wanted the case, like this one.

She should have gone directly to her private runabout and let one of her assistants clean up this mess. Even though no one on her staff had been cleared to handle all of the details in this case. She hadn't brought a lot onto the base; she had planned to work on the runabout, away from prying eyes.

The assistant could have cleaned up in no time. *She* could clean up in no time.

But she was just sitting at the desk, thinking thoughts she never normally had.

Like quitting the prosecutor's office altogether. Opening up her own defense practice. Starting with Jorja Lakinas, even though Lakinas had betrayed her. Maybe even stealing the defense case from whatsername Mukasey, just to show the upstarts here on this backwater starbase how real law was practiced.

Although Carbone probably wouldn't have been able to litigate that part of the case. She had seen the prosecution's files after all, and knew their strategy—or what they considered to be a strategy.

But she could take on Lakinas's medical case, and make the prosecution's case a living nightmare, figuring out ways to block anything the prosecution tried to do without being involved at all.

Then she let out a breath, put her hands in her hair and leaned forward, feeling exhausted.

She was being petty. Revenge usually wasn't her style—outside of the courtroom.

They had let her go, when she had fought against being removed as the lead on this case. She could fight the dismissal or she could acquiesce. If she fought it, then the case would be delayed, the judges would be annoyed, and she still had to litigate a case she would probably lose because of Lakinas and the five other defendants.

Carbone stood. She shouldn't have come. She should have said no in the first place. She had known this case would be dangerous for her. She should have listened to her own internal voice.

Instead, she had allowed herself to be persuaded. And that carefully cultivated reputation of hers was going to take a major hit.

Then she smiled. It would take a major hit if they controlled the message.

But she would do that. And she would do it with the truth.

They didn't like her plan for tackling the case. She had the only winning strategy, and they had turned it down.

She was going to wish them luck, while making sure that everyone knew the only person who could have won this case for the prosecution was Danitra Carbone—and they had let her go.

TWELVE

The interviews were difficult and gave her a headache. Mukasey insisted on doing the in-depth interviews herself; she wanted to make sure she didn't miss anything.

But she wasn't sure what she was missing. She listened to more than a hundred *Renegat* survivors and the first thing she learned was that these people had complaints about everything. Their accommodations, the fact that they had no real freedom, the way the Fleet was treating them.

She had hoped that talking to her assistants had gotten the complaints out of the defendants' systems, but no. Once they had a new audience, they began all over again.

And unless she wanted to piss them off, she had to listen, even though she didn't want to.

She conducted the interviews in a small conference room off her office. She probably should have conducted the interviews in the tower where the defendants were housed, but her assistants recommended that she give each defendant an outing. She had listened, and that, at least, had brought some gratitude.

Along with the food and beverages she had provided, which were different and apparently better than the food they could get onsite, she at least had some of the defendants smiling.

The rest were angry. Furiously angry. The kind of angry that radiated from the room outward.

She sat alone with them in the small room, and wished it was larger to let all of that emotion have some space. She sat on one side of a table that was nothing more than a table—no console for any kind of computer system, nothing that allowed her to record the conversations, no food delivery system built in. Not even a modified dumb waiter to remove dishes.

The table always threw interviewees for a loop, since they expected her to have more tech inside the room. She did—on the walls, three different systems recording every deposition, every interview—but none of the systems were visible. Not even her assistants knew about one of the systems. That one was just for her, and she often used it for staff relations.

The rest, though, usually had someone monitoring them. She liked having two pairs of eyes on a conversation—that way she didn't have to rewatch it, which she always felt was a waste of time. Two pairs of eyes, both familiar with the case, could often find several different things, and she found that helpful.

Especially in this case, in which none of the defendants were telling the same story. They all had had different experiences on the *Renegat*, and all of them were—as all defendants usually were—innocent, at least according to them.

She was inclined to believe that they had not participated in Nadim Crowe's actual mutiny. It seemed to have come from the engineering department, and with the exception of Kabac, who could prove he had been fired by Crowe as an engineer long before either of them ever made it onto the *Renegat*, not a single one of the 193 people who had survived ever served in engineering—even before Preemas had messed with everyone's job descriptions.

Most of the defendants so far had told tales of hiding during the worst of the fighting, or helping with the cleanup. A few claimed they had told Crowe no when he asked them to join him on the old Fleet ships he was refurbishing.

One person had told her that Crowe believed the *Renegat* would not make it back to the Fleet, ever, and he had tried to convince her to stay, based on that alone.

She had said he seemed panicked about it, but no one else had mentioned it.

Maybe Nadim Crowe was one of those people who played favorites. Maybe he had made that offer to a few people, but not all of them.

If he—as the chief engineer of the *Renegat*—believed the ship could not safely return to the Fleet, then why did he let them go?

As she worked her way through the interviews, she ended up with many more questions than answers. She had no sense of Preemas, for example. Most everyone said he was mercurial, but some thought he was a visionary while others believed he didn't care about anyone but himself.

She had dealt with other cases involving captains, and she knew that a lot of the perceptions were filtered through the interviewee's relationship to authority. Unfortunately, everyone on the *Renegat* had had bad experiences with authority, so they were all damaged in that area.

She saw it in the anger against the Fleet. She also saw it in anger against Preemas, for some of them, and for others, anger against Crowe.

This case was large, and she was having trouble finding the right angle on it.

And then there were the six people that Carbone had tried to break off from the investigation. They weren't quite Mukasey's ace in the hole, but they did negate the charges that the Fleet was trying to bring. They tried to prevent the mutiny. They tried to keep the *Renegat* alive.

No matter what information the six of them had, Mukasey wouldn't have been able to use it in court.

But they didn't have to announce Carbone's dismissal. They could have just sent her home, elevated Arias, and claimed that a different case had taken Carbone out of the jurisdiction. Or maybe that since the case was being tried in Starbase Sigma's court, they could have lied and said that Arias's experience in that court would have been sufficient for the case.

Instead, they were making a big deal out of the fact that Danitra Carbone was leaving and Abram Yglesias, whom everyone called the Old Man, had taken over.

That did make Mukasey sit up and take notice, because she couldn't remember the last time Yglesias tried a case. She had no idea what his style was, although legend had it that once upon a time, he made Carbone look like an amateur.

Mukasey didn't think Carbone made a big mistake. Not a firing mistake. She should have contacted Mukasey, of course, because she was meeting with one of Mukasey's clients. And the client should have notified her before the fact, not after. Carbone had also defied the order of the court that the defendants had to stay together.

But if Lakinas and the others had taken the pleas, the court would not have vacated them, based on procedure. The court would have looked the other way, and Mukasey's case would have been weakened.

That would have made a win for the prosecution almost inevitable.

And yet, they fired the most famous prosecutor in the Fleet.

Mukasey's brain was already filled with too many details. She didn't need this added wrinkle. It made her feel paranoid. It made her feel like she was missing something very, very important.

So she buried herself in the details from the defendants. The battle for the *Renegat*, the overuse of the brig. The ultimate investigation of the Scrapheap itself—as the *Renegat* had initially been assigned to do—along with the discovery that hundreds, maybe thousands, of ships had gone missing during the Scrapheap's lifetime.

That probably should not have been a surprise, but it was to some on the *Renegat*—and, probably was to the Fleet now. The Scrapheaps were considered protected space, filled with ruined and outmoded ships. The Scrapheaps were supposed to be impenetrable, and this one had not been. Its forcefield had been open to space, and a lot of items, not just ships, had gone missing.

And then, apparently, Crowe and his cronies had gone into the Scrapheap and found even more working ships. They had taken *anacapa* drives off of those ships, with the idea that the drives would replace damaged drives on the *Renegat*.

Then there had been some kind of meeting, in which Crowe demanded that everyone stay in that sector and never return to the Fleet. Some of the defendants said that Crowe had been belligerent when the crew told him they wanted to return to the Fleet.

Others claimed that he had replaced the *anacapa* drive with a working drive, and wished them luck.

Mukasey wasn't sure she believed either story. She wasn't sure she believed *any* of the stories, not really. Something in the way the stories got told made her think everyone was lying.

Everyone except Lakinas. Lakinas had said she hadn't known how decisions were made to return to the Fleet. She had been in the brig, along with her five compatriots. Others had been in the brig as well—at least that was the sense that Mukasey got from a few of the interviews she had conducted.

And then the speaker—whoever it was (and it didn't seem to matter who)—would give her a sideways look. They were lying, covering up something big—as if this case wasn't big enough—and she wasn't sure what that was.

She hoped her assistants would find something in the files she had received from the Fleet, files that had come from the *Renegat* before she exploded, but Mukasey wasn't holding her breath.

She wasn't sure if the ship continued to update its records after the knowledgeable crew left. That was the thing that shocked her the most about the *Renegat* defendants. They made it back without a lot of what the Fleet considered essential personnel.

And that was going to be front and center in her arguments against the mutiny charge. These people fought every step of the way to return home, so they should be allowed to live their lives.

She still had a lot of work to do before she made any arguments. Her nightmare was that she would still have mountains of data to go through the night before she had to give opening arguments. She couldn't afford to hire enough staff to go through everything rapidly. She didn't trust any specialized program to look for key concepts, incidents, or words—although she might be able to use that later. And she wasn't sure she trusted anyone else to figure out what she needed.

Yes, she had caught a break now that Carbone was gone. But it didn't feel like a win. It felt like a trap.

And she wasn't sure why.

She just needed to figure out what—if anything—the defendants were hiding, and how—if possible—she could use that information to win the case.

THIRTEEN

He wouldn't look at her. Not directly.

Jorja Lakinas hunched in her special chair and put her crabbed hand front and center. She had taken her time entering this office, her monitoring chip blinking green because she had permission to be in this part of Starbase Sigma.

This part was so different from the section she was currently living in.

After living mostly on what this culture she found herself in would consider "old" ships and after spending so much time on the *Renegat*, which even by her time's standard was an out-of-date vessel, the section of Starbase Sigma where she had been living seemed very modern.

But this section, with its recessed lighting and the way that the walls dampened sound unless she set her own internal controls to have certain sounds elevated—well, everything about this part of Starbase Sigma felt beyond modern. It felt almost unfamiliar, as if she had entered an alien culture.

Or it would have, if humans weren't the same everywhere.

And this attorney, this Oscar Vaas, he acted like everyone else who saw her for the first time. His first and only direct look began with eye contact and the beginning of a smile, and then he realized what he was seeing. His gaze slithered away, but not away far enough. He saw her crabbed hand, the cart, the way her body twisted, and then he realized that she had seen him look away, and that he would embarrass himself if he looked even farther away, but he couldn't stop himself.

His gaze found the floor, then the wall, then maybe the door, as he hoped someone, anyone, would save him from this meeting. But he had no one, because he had no human assistant. He only had the system he had set up to give his clients privacy, or so his information had said.

When Jorja researched him she found his interest in privacy perfectly suited to her. She didn't want to answer questions from other people about why she was getting her own attorney. She didn't want to answer to the Fleet or to her so-called colleagues.

She wanted to take care of herself.

"You know who I am, right?" she asked in the most forceful voice she had.

His shoulders straightened. She could actually see him put himself together. The office was small, but tastefully decorated—lots of holographic depictions of mountains from places she did not recognize as well as some images of mountain lakes rotating in and out. The office itself smelled faintly of fresh pine and lake water, something he must have paid dearly for.

At least he had room for her cart. The chairs he had for clients had moved to the side of the wall as she wheeled herself into the antechamber.

That little move alone led her to believe that he had represented someone like her before.

But she shouldn't assume.

His gaze met hers. He had very green eyes which looked like emeralds in his light brown skin. He had tight black curls that fell against his face as if he had designed them that way—and maybe he had.

He was the kind of man who knew he was handsome, and, she suspected, he was the kind of lawyer who used his good looks to his advantage.

The power of his gaze held her—or maybe it wasn't the power of his gaze at all. Maybe it was the fact that almost no one in this godforsaken place ever looked her in the face.

The novelty of it hit her like a blow.

"I know who you are," he said. "I researched you. And if you're here to have me work with Eun Ae Mukasey, I won't, not without her permission."

"That's a different case," Jorja said.

His eyebrows went up, a movement she suspected was deliberate, because he had a great reputation as a lawyer. Most lawyers she met could hide their emotions completely.

"I'm here because I want to sue the Fleet," she said.

He tilted his head a little, as if he hadn't expected that. He was a good actor, she would have to give him that. Or maybe he really was surprised at everything she was saying.

He had expected her to hire him to represent her on the mutiny charges, after all.

"Do you mind if I sit?" He waved a hand toward a small desk that had been lost in the pile of furniture in the corner.

"It's your office." She didn't want to give an opinion on what he could or couldn't do. Nor did she want to reveal everything she was feeling.

She hated it when people stood over her. They *loomed*, and she hated that more than almost anything. But she'd learned to hide it, because when people saw that she was uncomfortable, they assumed she was in pain.

He waved a hand, and the desk, along with one of the chairs, glided toward him. Jorja couldn't see the rails or whatever they were that brought the pieces of furniture close, but she did feel the floor vibrate slightly.

This man had made a lot of money in his work; she knew that because he hadn't come from money. All that he had, he had earned himself.

That was encouraging.

"People don't generally sue the Fleet," he said. "The Fleet provides our lives, our homes, our income. We live here and we are subject to them and what they do. Any lawsuits against the Fleet generally come from sector bases, where people can go off and live on their own, without Fleet contact."

She felt a slight surge of irritation. She should have been used to this kind of over-explaining by now. It had started when she had gotten injured, and it never stopped.

"People don't generally get denied medical care, not once, not twice, but three times, by the Fleet." She let just a bit of the anger she was feeling into her voice.

His gaze went up and down her entire body. This time, there was no shame in his look and no judgement. There was just a clear assessment of everything he was looking at.

"Your injuries come from the *Renegat?*" he asked. "From the rescue?"

"From what that woman they fired from the prosecution case…" she took a deliberate breath to see if he knew who she was referring to.

"Danitra Carbone," he said.

Jorja inclined her head once. An acknowledgement, nothing more.

"…what she called the battle for the *Renegat*. When we were fighting to prevent Nadim Crowe from taking over the ship."

"You were on the side of the dead captain, Preemas?" Vaas asked.

"I fought for the ship, yes," she said, being very careful. She hadn't liked Preemas. By the end, no one had. But she had believed that he was the only one who could get them to the Scrapheap, and then get them home.

She had been wrong.

"We lost," she said fairly quickly, because she didn't want to discuss the "battle for the *Renegat*" or Carbone or Preemas for that matter. "While others got taken to the med bay, I was sent to the brig. No one took care of my wounds."

"Do you mind if I record?" he asked.

"I thought you already were," she said.

"Not without express permission." He smiled at her. "You learn in my profession that if you follow the rules to the letter, you usually can't get nailed on technicalities."

She smiled in return. Her skin stretched painfully across her jawline and cheekbones. She didn't smile often, not only because she looked horrible doing so, but because it hurt.

His fingers moved across the top of his desk. "Repeat what you just said."

She did.

"Do you have any idea why you were not taken to the med bay?" he asked.

"Someone told me later they were triaging. But even after the triage ended, no one took care of me," she said. "I got some minor treatment, but it wasn't until Crowe had left the ship that I actually got real medical care."

Vaas raised his head. "I'm not up on the details of what happened at that Scrapheap," he said.

"I'm not going to go into them right now," she said. "Not until I know you can represent me."

"Suing the Fleet…" He let the words hang. "That's a tall order."

She nodded. "I'm not done."

"All right," he said.

"I got some care from the team after we started back home," she said. "But we didn't have any real medical experts. They could just use the equipment to patch me up. No real repair."

He nodded.

"Then we got rescued—" and she wasn't going to tell him about that.

Everyone, it seemed, knew about the rescue of the *Renegat.* It had happened quickly and efficiently, saving a lot of lives, because the *Renegat*'s *anacapa* drive had finally failed, and the ship blew up. There was footage of the rescue. There was a lot of interest in it, and the survivors. The news stories never stopped. The requests for interviews never ended.

But once the Fleet decided to charge the entire surviving crew with mutiny, then the Fleet also denied access to the crew members.

"—and I thought that was when I'd get real medical care," she said.

"Were you injured in the rescue?" he asked.

The question made her furious. What did it matter? But it probably did. She was hiring a lawyer, not a mental health consultant.

"How am I supposed to know?" she asked. "I was already injured. Did it get worse? I don't know. Did it hurt, that rescue? Like hell."

He tilted his head. The assessment was clearly continuing.

"And when I got here, I asked for repair. Everyone gets repair. *Everyone* who serves with the Fleet knows that their injuries get repaired after something awful. But no. I got some minor treatment, but no repair. I was given this—" She waved her hand at the cart. "—and a room designed for people who aren't really mobile, and that's it."

His eyes had become hooded, probably so that she couldn't see his emotional reaction.

She leaned forward, even though it hurt her twisted spine.

"I am a *loyal* member of the Fleet. I deserve proper medical care. It is clear to me that they decided *before* they opened the mutiny case, that I was guilty of something, so they did not even try to make me better." She lowered her voice, so that her fury wasn't quite as evident. "I deserve to be better."

"Fascinating," he said.

Now her anger rose, almost uncontrollably. "Fascinating? This is my life we're discussing."

"It is," he said. "But 'want,' 'need,' 'deserve,' those are words that aren't going to get us anywhere."

"Us?" she asked. Did that mean he was going to take the case? She felt a little glimmer of hope, something she hadn't felt since they emerged from foldspace in near Sector Base Z just before the *Renegat* blew up.

"Us," he said. "I'll take the case."

She let out a small sigh. "I have a lot of data on what I need—"

"'Need,'" he repeated. "That's irrelevant."

She bristled.

"They're not going to listen to what someone needs, particularly when they've made up their mind about you." He waved a hand. "I believe that. I've believed that since I started following the mutiny case."

"You're following it?" she asked. "Why?"

"Because the legal community here is small," he said, "and I have learned on high-profile cases that it's best to pay attention, in case you're called in at the last minute to take over for someone else."

She blinked, thought, then nodded. That made sense to her.

"Do I have to sign something?" she asked.

"We've recorded the agreement," he said. "We'll do more, but right now, that'll cover both of us."

"Except that you have the recording," she said.

"I'll make sure you have a copy," he said.

Her heart started pounding, hard. She didn't want to wait.

"You're going to have to trust me if we work together," he said. "And I understand. After all that's happened to you, you don't trust easily."

She had been about to say that, but she wasn't going to admit it.

"What about 'obligation'?" she asked. "Will that get the Fleet to take care of me?"

"That and publicity might be the route a lesser lawyer would take," he said. "And we might have to. But I'm looking at this with a slightly different eye."

She frowned. That movement didn't hurt as much as smiling did.

"Meaning what?" she asked.

"Meaning we need leverage, and they have a high-profile case against you *Renegat* survivors, a case they want to win," he said.

A chill ran down her aching back. She didn't trust him, not really. She could barely breathe, afraid he was going to say something stupid.

"Do you have something?" he asked. "Information? Anything that would help the Fleet win their case?"

She closed her eyes. Betrayal. All these lawyers wanted was to get someone to betray their friends.

She opened her eyes. She sighed, and was about to tell him he'd been fired, when he raised a hand.

"Listen to me," he said. "The information has to be true. It needs to be verifiable. And it can remain secret."

That caught her. "What do you mean, secret?" she asked.

"We will negotiate with them. They will provide you with medical care in exchange for some major piece of verifiable—from another source, verifiable—information. We will ask that your case be dealt with privately. There will be signed nondisclosure agreements, binding on them as well as us."

"They'll do that?" she asked.

He nodded.

"What if I have to testify?" she asked.

"You wouldn't," he said. "That's why it's verifiable. We'd ask them to drop the charges against you, based on your medical condition. You're in no shape to go to a Fleet penitentiary."

Another shiver ran down her spine. She hadn't even thought about what might happen to her if everyone was found guilty.

"You'd be separated out. We'd send you to a different starbase to get medical care, and then no one would see you again." He folded his hands in front of him. "Would that work for you?"

She took a deep breath. They weren't really her friends. Not close friends, anyway. And she wanted a new life. And, damn, she wanted the pain to end. She wanted people to look her in the face. She wanted to move easily, without reaching for something to brace herself with every step.

Was it betrayal if they didn't know she had done it?

"Yes," she said quietly. "That would work for me."

He gave her a small smile. "We'll need to solidify our relationship," he said. "I'll set it up for the Fleet to pay me, if we can get them to agree."

"If?" she asked.

"If," he said. "Because what they'll do will depend on the quality of your information. If it will change the case or move it in their favor, then they'll be a lot more willing to give us everything we want. Would the information you have do that?"

She smiled again, despite the pain. What she had would shake the case from top to bottom. Would it help the Fleet? She didn't know. She wasn't a lawyer. But it certainly would not help the crew members of the now-defunct *Renegat*.

"Yes," she said. "The information I have will change everything."

FOURTEEN

Mukasey paced her small office, holoscreens floating around her. She had nearly fallen asleep at her desk while working on this case, so she had taken to standing now. She was used to working hard, but what she had to do here was nearly impossible, especially with her few resources.

She'd spent the week interviewing the defendants, and had learned nothing, except one thing she didn't want to learn.

They were hiding something, something that had happened at that Scrapheap. Whenever she pushed them about the events that sent them back to Sector Base Z, they changed the subject or looked away or gave her vague answers.

She might have left it alone if it weren't for the fact that the decision to return seemed crucial. Half, or maybe more, of the crew remained at that Scrapheap. This crew came back with the *Renegat*.

She didn't believe the amiable split story, but she couldn't find anything to disprove it—well, except for the battle for the *Renegat.* But that happened long before the crew split and half remained.

She needed to pressure them, but the only way she knew how to do that was with evidence, which meant she had to comb through the records pulled off the *Renegat* before it was destroyed. There was so much information, even though some of it had been scrubbed.

Usually, though, in her experience, she had learned that scrubbing left traces. Normally, she would hire someone to go through the material with her, to figure out what was missing. She had a service that could find the bits and pieces from the scrubbings.

In theory, that service kept confidentiality, but she wasn't sure it would on this case. The case was too big, and there were media outlets that were willing to pay to get all kinds of information on the *Renegat* Renegades. Her meager payments wouldn't counteract someone else's greed, particularly if that person could cover their tracks well enough.

Since she would be hiring the service to comb through databases, she figured leaking the information without a trace would be in their skill set.

She couldn't take the risk.

She was doing so much of this alone that she was skimping on sleep. She had done that as a young lawyer, but it was harder as an older one. Hence the pacing. It kept her from dozing off.

She would have to sleep soon enough, though.

Mukasey pulled the screen toward herself. On it was the judge who had recused herself. She had a strong chin, clear eyes, and papery skin covered with faint lines.

An old woman, then, without a lot of vanity. Her black hair was streaked with silver. Something in her expression made her seem ageless, but Mukasey knew she had to be older. She had had a conflict of interest in the *Renegat* case, after all.

The image had biographical information attached, but Mukasey's eyes had gone too blurry to read it. She really would have to sleep soon. She wasn't making much progress at all anymore.

She commanded the holoscreen to read the information to her.

A programmed gender-neutral voice read in a flat tone.

Admiral Bella Gão, Retired, is well known throughout the sector for her charitable works. The work includes…

"Skip the charities," Mukasey said. Being tired also made her impatient. If there was something in that information, she would look later.

Since her retirement, Admiral Gão has taken a second career as a tribunal judge. She sits on two or more tribunals per year, and her opinions are quoted throughout—

"Skip the tribunals," Mukasey said. Most of the judges had gone to school for this second career. The language she had heard in that section was similar to the information about the other judges.

Before her retirement, Admiral Gão spent decades in active duty for the Fleet.

That caught Mukasey's attention. One hundred years?

The changes Admiral Gão championed saved hundreds of lives. She also influenced the way that Scrapheaps were run, updating the program and make it more efficient. Her work—

"Wait," Mukasey said. "Pause."

She leaned into the screen, no longer as tired as she had been. She scanned the information, looking for the words Scrapheap. Some of the changes were so high-level that she couldn't access them, but some were common-sense.

Such as this: Gão stopped the practice of sending a single ship back to investigate problems with a Scrapheap. Gão ultimately managed to get the Fleet to send a small group of ships to any Scrapheap in distress. She also set up a team to facilitate communication across long distances, and through foldspace itself.

The hair stood up on the back of Mukasey's neck.

Mukasey put in a request for Gão's personnel record, and that request was immediately denied.

Mukasey took a deep breath. She needed to do this slowly, and by the book. There was something here; that was obvious. She just had to figure out what it was, without putting her clients in any jeopardy, without hurting her case, and without tipping off the Fleet itself.

Tall order. Tall enough that she couldn't do it on no sleep. She would make possibly fatal mistakes.

She needed to get some sleep. Then she needed to track down information on Admiral Bella Gão, Retired.

Because Gão knew something. Something important.

And Mukasey needed to know it as well.

FIFTEEN

One of the defendants wanted to talk to the Old Man. That peaked Arias's interest. Apparently, it peaked the Old Man's too, because he was going to hold the meeting, in the office he had initially set aside for Carbone.

Arias still worked in the side office. Both she and the Old Man used Carbone's old office for evidence, files, locked tablets and the ever-mushrooming data from this never-ending case.

And, of course, the Old Man had moved an ancient, rather cruddy couch in here. Arias had slept on it too many times already. Her back complained each and every time.

She brought a cup of coffee into the office. They were going to meet with the lawyer first—the Old Man's strategy. He really didn't want to see the defendant first, poke around and try to figure out what that person had to offer.

When Arias asked why, the Old Man's answer was simple. *We're trying a case against 193 people. I think of them as a unit. I don't want to see individuals.*

She had nodded, then thought about that for nearly a day afterward. That was the better strategy. Individual parts of that unit might have done something—the way a hand grasped a weapon—but that hand still belonged to the body as a whole.

His simple statement had transformed the way she had been looking at this case. It had been complex enough, just trying to figure out who had done what, when, and how.

While she had dug through the information, she had worried that she might put too much blame on one individual, not enough on another. She had worried that the tribunal would force her to separate the cases, which meant she would have to make deals with some and try some of the worst actors.

But if she rigidly held to the fact that they were all a unit, she had a greater chance of winning this thing.

She wished that the Old Man had told her that strategy from the start. Then she realized why he hadn't. He had thought she already knew it.

The more she worked with him, the more she realized that he thought her more capable than she thought herself.

He was sitting behind the desk, almost still. The Old Man was never still. His chair was tilted backwards, and his feet were crossed on top of the desk. He had a tablet before him, and he was scrolling through it.

His right forefingers tapped a slight rhythm on the chair's arm. She half-smiled when she saw the movement. Never still.

"They want something from us," he said without looking up.

"Obviously," Arias said.

"No, not obvious," the Old Man said. "I've been looking up this lawyer, this Vaas. You know him?"

"Yeah," Arias said. "I won a personal injury against him."

It was rare for prosecutors in her office to take on a personal injury case. She had acted as the defendant's attorney in this one, since the accused was the Fleet.

Usually, personal injury cases didn't happen on bases like Starbase Sigma. Injuries and the complaints were handled inside the Fleet. But this had been a civilian who had fallen off a ramp in the docking bay, and had slammed his head against a railing, resulting in actual brain damage. The injury was reparable, even though the civilian had lingering symptoms. The Fleet had even paid for the medical, just as a matter of course, but the civilian wanted personal damages.

The Fleet didn't do damages. The Fleet rarely thought about money at all. That was for non-Fleet bases and other cultures. The civilian hadn't realized that—and Vaas had clearly taken the case to see if he could open a small hole in the Fleet's very firm stance against damage payments for civilians.

It hadn't worked, primarily because Arias had argued to that tribunal that opening the door would change the very heart of the Fleet itself. Privately, she had always thought the civilian had a real argument. Not that real arguments mattered in a court of law.

"I remember that thing," the Old Man said, without looking up from his tablet. "Well argued on both sides. Aspirational on his part. This guy is ambitious."

The Old Man didn't say that in admiration, but instead, like it was something they could use.

"He's not working with Mukasey," the Old Man said. "He's on his own."

"He wants something specific for his client," Arias said. "I suspect I even know who the client is."

"Lakinas?" the Old Man asked.

Arias nodded. "I think Carbone put an idea in her head, and she went after a good attorney to get whatever she needs."

"Let's see what she's got to trade," the Old Man said. He set the tablet down.

"You handling the negotiation or am I?" Arias asked.

He looked at her sideways. "You think she has something?"

Arias shrugged one shoulder. "Vaas does. If she didn't, he would have sent her back to Mukasey."

"Good point," the Old Man said. "He thinks he's meeting with me, but I'll defer to you. He'll probably think you're my second—"

"That's all right," Arias said. "Everyone's terrified of you."

The Old Man barked a laugh. Then a small chime rang. Someone who didn't belong in the office had arrived.

"You ready for this?" he asked.

"As I'll ever be," she said. She took the chair he had placed on the corner of the desk, on his side. There was one more chair in front of the desk, because they had expressly told Vaas not to bring his client.

The nice thing about Vaas was that he didn't play games. He would play by the rules, knowing that most attorneys lost by aggravating their opponents and forcing rules violations to become issues, rather than handling something on its merits.

The door opened, and Vaas stepped inside. He was a ridiculously handsome man, whose square chin accented not just his entire face, but the broadness of his shoulders and the military trim to his body. He had been Fleet—they had all been Fleet—but he had left the Fleet so that he could practice the kind of law he liked.

His gaze met Arias's first. Those green eyes always startled her. They were serious now, and he seemed just a bit nervous. There was actual gel in his black curls. It glistened. He wore a silver-gray tunic that looked almost martial over black pants. It made him look official, which he might have needed for his own confidence.

Yes indeed. The Old Man intimidated everyone.

The Old Man pretended not to notice. He waved a hand at the empty chair. "Have a seat."

Vaas nodded, then sat, almost like a child expecting to be disciplined. He clutched a single tablet and set it gingerly on his lap. He almost seemed nervous.

The Old Man said nothing. He just waited. It was an old tactic of his, one that Arias had stolen years ago. Most people were very uncomfortable with silence.

Because she had worked with the Old Man her entire career, she was not. So she sat beside him, and waited.

Vaas glanced at her. She raised her eyebrows, encouraging him to speak.

"I'm…ah…representing Jorja Lakinas," he said.

So they were right. The woman that Carbone had tried to turn to their side now wanted something, through her own lawyer.

"Why isn't Mukasey here?" Arias asked.

Vaas shot her an irritated glance. Apparently, he thought that he would talk only to the Old Man.

"Because I'm Jorja's lawyer," he said.

"So is she," Arias said. "At least, last we heard."

"This is a different issue," Vaas said.

"Then it has nothing to do with us," Arias said.

"It has to do with her injuries." Vaas turned slightly away from her and spoke directly to the Old Man. "She wants compensation."

The Old Man made a small movement with his right hand, so small that Arias doubted Vaas could see it. It meant: Let me talk.

"This office offered her the opportunity to have her injuries repaired," the Old Man said. "She declined."

"Hmmm," Vaas said. "I hadn't realized that she had spoken to your office. I thought Danitra Carbone had spoken to her personally."

"Danitra Carbone represented our office at the time," the Old Man said.

Arias had to work not to smile. The Old Man had been furious with Carbone when the offer happened. He wouldn't have acknowledged her work then.

"That offer," the Old Man said, "had a shelf-life. It lasted for the duration of that particular meeting."

"And I'm not here about that offer." Vaas's voice had grown stronger. He was getting more comfortable. "Jorja Lakinas hired me to help her force the Fleet to meet its obligations and care for her health."

The Old Man made that ever-so-slight movement again, this time giving Arias permission to take over the meeting again.

"Again," Arias said. "That's not our issue. You'll have to bring the suit, and see what happens with whatever tribunal you get assigned."

"I would rather avoid a tribunal," Vaas said.

"Most of us would," Arias said. "But we usually don't get what we want."

"I told Jorja that I would talk to you before I brought any action against the Fleet," Vaas said.

"Now you have," Arias said. "You can return to your client with a clear conscience."

Vaas shot her another irritated glance. "We would like to bargain with you."

"Our theory of the case has changed," the Old Man said. He spoke before Arias could. Apparently he wasn't going to be as silent as he had said he would. "Danitra Carbone was pursuing leads that no longer interest us."

"I am aware of that," Vaas said. "We don't want that deal. We would like to trade crucial information for Jorja's repair and rehabilitation. We would also like to have her salary reinstated, and give her the retirement benefits promised to anyone who voluntarily leaves the Fleet."

"No," the Old Man said.

"You haven't even heard what she has to offer," Vaas said.

"I don't need to," the Old Man said. "We will not give her a salary or retirement. Nor will we reinstate her. Not for any reason."

Arias noted that he had left out the health benefits, and if she noticed, she was sure Vaas had as well.

She also understood why the Old Man was so adamant about not reinstating Lakinas. That would set a precedent. It would treat Lakinas like an individual instead of part of the unit. Giving her health benefits could be argued as compassionate care, something that Fleet regulations allowed under many circumstances, although none as extreme as this one.

"You might, after you hear what she has to offer," Vaas said.

"No," the Old Man said. "We will not. If that's what brought you, then thank you, but we're not interested. Now, if you'll excuse us, we have a case to work on—"

"You'll want her information." Vaas sounded a little desperate. He thought whatever she had was good. He clearly hadn't expected to be shut down immediately.

"We don't need it," Arias said. "We have images of the battle for the *Renegat*. We have witness logs and medical histories. We have interviews and more information than we can actually use at trial."

"I'm sure you do." Vaas's lips moved in a perfunctory smile, one that didn't reach those amazing green eyes. "However, you don't have what she can give you."

Before she spoke, Arias made sure she sounded very dismissive. "Oh?" she asked. "And what's that?"

"The fate of Nadim Crowe," Vaas said. "The true fate, not the lies you're being told."

Arias's heartrate jumped. She hoped her surprise didn't show on her face.

"What happened to him?" she asked, keeping her voice flat.

"No," Vaas said, and this time, he looked at the Old Man. In fact, Vaas had imitated the Old Man's tone. "This time, I get to draw the line. You will make an agreement with me and then you will hear Lakinas's statement."

"No." The Old Man swung his legs off the desk. "It doesn't work that way. We hear what she says, we corroborate it, and if it we think we can use it, *then* we make a deal."

Vaas was shaking his head.

"That's all you get," the Old Man said. "Jorja Lakinas and her colleagues have lied to us from the beginning of this case. We have no reason to believe anything she says. We will not make a deal with someone we know to be a serial liar, not without the opportunity to verify her information."

"There's no way to verify," Vaas said. "The records are gone. Which is why you're having trouble on this very point, aren't you?"

"It's no good to us if we can't verify," Arias said.

"Oh, don't give me that, Lucinda," Vaas said. "I've stood toe-to-toe with you. You're a better lawyer than that."

A surge of anger flooded her, which was probably what he wanted. But she managed to keep her face impassive.

"You use this information against any of the *Renegat* Renegades in court, and they will crack," Vaas said.

"They're not going to be placed on the stand," Arias said. "You know that."

"They will if you call them," Vaas said. "We want Jorja's health benefits, repair and rehabilitation, as promised to every Fleet cadet from time immemorial. And she will not testify. She will give you the information under oath, but she won't speak in front of the court."

"No," the Old Man said.

Vaas's cheeks grew noticeably darker. He was getting angry. "Then we have no choice but to sue the Fleet."

"Good luck with that," the Old Man said. "You will lose. The case will wait until ours is done, and when we win, she will get nothing."

He placed his feet ostentatiously on the desk again, then crossed his hands over his stomach.

"Good day," he said.

Vaas stood. He started for the door, then stopped. "You'll want this information."

"We don't need it," Arias said.

"Oh, but you do," Vaas said. His eyes moved ever so slightly. It was a tell. He was thinking about how to salvage this interview. "Crowe and his colleagues are most likely dead."

Arias's heart rate increased again. She hoped she didn't have as obvious a tell as Vaas.

"Of course they are," she said. "They are at least one hundred years in the past. Some of them would be well past two hundred now."

Vaas shook his head. "No. They most likely died shortly after the *Renegat* left that Scrapheap."

"Most likely is not the same as definitely," Arias said.

The Old Man raised that hand, this time so that Vaas could see it. "How can she assume that they're dead?"

Vaas almost smiled, but caught himself before the smile had room to grow. Still, Arias saw it, and if she had, then the Old Man had too.

"Because they didn't have enough supplies to make it for very long," Vaas said.

"I thought they chose to leave the *Renegat*," Arias said.

"Who told you that?" Vaas asked. "The *Renegat* Renegades?"

Yes. They had told everyone that story. Or a version of it. But she didn't answer.

"Jorja has that information. She knows what happened. She's willing to tell you in granular detail. She has personal notes from the *Renegat*, which were rescued with her. You might be able to confirm some of the information, just by comparing the ship's stores before they arrived at the Scrapheap with the stores after they left. You have that information, right?"

Probably not. But Arias wasn't going to tell him about the gaps in the records. Although most of those records had vanished from the logs. Would the defendants have been smart enough to delete information such as the amount of food stores? She doubted it.

"This is vague," the Old Man said. "She would have to testify."

"No," Vaas said. "She's adamant about not testifying."

The Old Man shrugged. "Then she won't get her repair and rehabilitation."

"She doesn't want the others to know that she spoke to you about this," Vaas said.

"Then we'll see which part of her wins," the Old Man said. "We'll listen to her. If we like what we hear, then we will make an offer. That offer will include testimony."

Vaas shook his head. "She won't."

"Too bad," the Old Man said. "Thank you so much for your time."

Vaas didn't move. The Old Man made a small dismissive wave with his right hand.

"What if I can convince her to testify?" Vaas said.

"Then she gets repair and physical rehabilitation. Nothing more."

"What about the mutiny charges?" Vaas asked. "Would they be dropped? She fought alongside Captain Preemas, after all."

"We'd have to hear what she has to offer," the Old Man said. "We might let her serve her time in some kind of rehab facility, instead of prison."

"I'll take it to her," Vaas said. He sounded almost excited.

"You do that," the Old Man said.

Arias stood. She was going to escort Vaas out that door, if he wouldn't leave on his own.

But he got the hint. He left, pulling the door closed behind him.

"Your office," the Old Man said before Arias could speak. "We haven't swept this place."

He actually thought Vaas might try to bug the office of the prosecutors? Vaas was too good a lawyer for that. But, Arias knew, the Old Man had seen a lot in his time, so she humored him.

She walked into her office. He followed her, and pulled the door closed.

The office felt tiny in comparison to the main room, especially with the Old Man's large presence filling it.

"What do you think?" he asked.

"We can verify supplies," Arias said. "I doubt they were savvy enough to fix that."

"It's not enough," the Old Man said. "We would need her testimony to lay the groundwork."

"It might be enough," Arias said. "If we play it right. We'd have to wait for the right moment."

Then she smiled at him.

"But I've worked opposite Vaas," she said. "He wanted to leave with a deal. She wants to talk to us."

"You think she will?" the Old Man asked.

"If I tell Vaas that I'm going to leak his involvement to the other defendants, she just might," Arias said. "She knows they'd see her as a betrayer in either case."

The Old Man nodded slowly. "Don't you find it fascinating that she is worried about being perceived as a betrayer? She has already betrayed her oath to the Fleet, and she helped make war against her crewmates."

Arias hadn't thought of that. But Lakinas had paid a huge price for her fight against her crewmates. Her entire body no longer functioned the way it had before.

Maybe she was terrified of being hurt again.

The Old Man looked at her, his eyes alight with interest. "You have an idea."

"Yes, I do," she said. "Vaas is right; all we have to do is call one or two of their people to testify. I can accuse, especially if we have information about the stores or some other supplies. We could see what happens there."

"I doubt we'll be able to get any of them to testify," the Old Man said.

"Let's see what happens," Arias said. "We might not need any of them."

"You still think Lakinas wants to talk with us," the Old Man said.

"She had time to think about Carbone's offer. Lakinas knows she can be a lot healthier with the Fleet's help. She has a huge incentive to help us and very little incentive to remain with that group." Arias nodded, feeling a confidence she hadn't felt before. "Yes, I think she'll talk with us. And if we can prove any part of what she says, then we have more than enough to win this case."

"A group murder," the Old Man said. "Who would have thought?"

"Murder will be hard to prove," Arias said. "But a careless disregard for others? That won't be hard at all."

"We haven't won this thing yet," the Old Man cautioned.

"I know," Arias said with a bit of a smile. "But we're a whole lot closer than we were."

SIXTEEN

Admiral Bella Gão, Retired, stared at the summons that flashed red on her screen. She could deny it. She was a sitting judge who handled several cases every year. She had already cited conflict of interest as her reason for refusing to sit on the *Renegat* case. She simply needed a point of privilege to refuse now, and the sitting twelve-judge panel would grant it to her.

She stood in the living room of her large apartment in a private sector of Starbase Sigma. She had had this apartment for eighty years. She'd redecorated twice, the last time ten years ago, moving most of her important items to the lower level. She added a bedroom down there as well.

She was ancient—her word, not anyone else's. She had retired from her admiralty over eighty-five years ago, after a long and full career. She had then returned to school with the Fleet's permission, learning the ins and outs of Fleet law so that she could sit on tribunals. She'd sat on hundreds of them in the intervening years. These days, she only took two or three cases per year, but in the early years of her retirement, after she had completed her schooling, she had sat on as many tribunals as possible.

She had liked the work—she still liked the work—and she was good at it. Yes, she was deciding life or death issues, but not in the same way that she had as an admiral. Now, she dealt with problems after they occurred. Before, she often caused some of the problems herself.

And that was one reason why she didn't even want to think about the *Renegat*.

She had been the one to staff up the ship, she had approved Captain Ivan Preemas for that mission, and she was the one who had believed Nadim Crowe when he had come to her with his concerns. The *Renegat* still haunted her, even now that it had returned.

Especially now that it had returned, with only part of its crew intact —and none of the people she had met before the ship went on its ill-fated mission.

She hadn't been surprised that it arrived one hundred years in its future. She had been worried about the effect of foldspace on that ship from the beginning. For years, she thought it had been lost in a foldspace bubble, its crew gone.

When the ship arrived and promptly blew up, part of her wondered if that explosion had been planned. She had researched enough to discover that it had not been planned; the ship was in such severe distress that it wouldn't have survived another foldspace jump. The crew had been lucky to make it.

Lucky and unlucky. They certainly hadn't planned on the time loss, nor had they foreseen the reaction to their arrival.

The *Renegat* had been a doomed ship from the start, and she had been part of that, even though she had regretted that involvement almost from the beginning.

She sat in the small study near the "new" bedroom. The study was the only room that hadn't gotten touched in the last redesign. The study was still modeled on her study on the *Správa* where she had last served as admiral. She had loved that study.

She loved this one as well, although not as much. It was smaller, here, and the furniture was a little too comfortable. She had a large overstuffed chair that had molded itself to her body, a pull-out desk that appeared when she needed it, and holographic tools that had been state-of-the-art when she had first moved into this apartment.

She had newer equipment in her living room/kitchen area. State-of-the-art equipment, in fact, but she preferred the older equipment. She also needed it because she still sometimes reviewed the files she had brought with her from the *Správa.* Maybe she had always known this moment would come for her.

The *Renegat* was her biggest mistake—and her biggest regret.

She could have stopped this entire trial, citing the original classification of the mission. It had been top secret back in its day. Now, no one cared, but then, that had been important.

Top-secret missions were rarely the subject of show trials, which was what this seemed to be trending to. Not because of the lawyers involved: they were all good at their jobs, at least now that Danitra Carbone was off the case. That woman had destroyed more good decisions with her bad ones than any other lawyer of Gāo's acquaintance.

The quality of the lawyers was what kept Gāo silent. There needed to be a true investigation of the *Renegat*, and the only way to get that at this late date was through the rigors of a trial. Otherwise, the Fleet had no reason to look at yet another failure, particularly one that involved foldspace and Scrapheaps.

Her involvement with the *Renegat* had allowed her to change a lot of policies to deal with Scrapheaps. She finally got the Fleet to remove Ready Vessels from the Scrapheaps. There was no reason to leave high-end ships in a hard-to-find protected area of any Scrapheap. The Fleet rarely retraced its steps, almost always moving forward. The people left behind on Sector Bases were on those bases voluntarily, preferring to live planetside. Even if a major war started in the sector, they would never again take to space.

The Ready Vessels were, in her opinion then and now, a danger to the Fleet. Some rogue operatives could find them, access them, and use them to come after the Fleet.

Part of her wondered if that was why Nadim Crowe had chosen to stay behind. He could build his own Fleet with the Ready Vessels in that abandoned Scrapheap.

Or so she hoped.

But from what little she had discovered through the media reports, the idea that Crowe had voluntarily stayed behind seemed shaky at best. No one really talked about it.

In fact, there weren't a lot of details at all.

She would get all the details she needed if she testified. The lawyer for the defense, Mukasey, was fishing right now; she wanted to know why Gão had recused herself. It could be easily explained by Gão's involvement in choosing the crew, and sending them all to that ancient Scrapheap, even though she had never believed in the mission.

She stared at the summons, thinking about her choices. She could refuse, but she wouldn't. She could simply answer questions and not provide much information at all.

She could tell this Mukasey why her clients were chosen to crew that ship, and what the expectations were. Gão could also tell Mukasey what changes the loss of the *Renegat* had wrought throughout the Fleet.

Or Gão could give her all of the information, the last images of Nadim Crowe, the discussions with Ivan Preemas, the logs she had made as her own nervousness grew. She could show the information she had received decades later from the Scrapheap itself.

She could confess to her mistakes in a public forum, and maybe, just maybe that would take some of the guilt from her shoulders.

Or maybe it would destroy the reputation she had painstakingly built over her very long life.

She sank into her overstuffed chair, tempted to call up that old holo of Nadim Crowe. But she had watched it so many times she had it memorized.

She leaned forward. She really didn't care about her reputation. Maybe if she was still a young woman, or still had a career in the admiralty, she might care.

She sighed. She owed Nadim Crowe one last hearing. His words needed to become public. He was being tried without the ability to defend himself—and everyone was entitled to a strong defense.

She let herself out of her study, and answered the request for the interview. Although she told Mukasey that the discussion would take place in Gão's apartment. That way, Gão could show Mukasey the recordings. All of them.

Let Mukasey decide how to use them.

That was how trials worked, after all.

SEVENTEEN

Trials were like sporting events. Eventually, time just ran out. Only unlike a sporting event, where the time ran out at the end, in a trial, the time ran out before the trial started. The research had to be finished or abandoned by the trial's beginning because the activity in court would become too all-consuming for the level of research that prepping for something this big usually took.

Arias always found the lack of time frustrating. Particularly when she knew she had to argue much of the case. Arguing the case meant she couldn't skimp too much on sleep. She didn't dare lose her train of thought.

She had to be interesting throughout the trial, because the twelve judges thought they had heard everything before. They would look away, or begin tapping on a screen built into the long bench before them, maybe already writing notes for their eventual contribution to the opinion.

Arias used to play sports when she was younger, and she had always been acutely aware that if she added a half an hour or subtracted an hour, the score would be different, and often a different team would win.

It was the same with research. She not only needed to know almost everything, but she needed all of that everything at her fingertips. Or, more accurately, in the file folders inside her mind. The tablets she brought to court had everything, even the unsorted research. She just had to know what fact she needed when and where, and how to insert it —with full logic and clarity—into her part of the case.

Usually, she could do that, but usually, she wasn't handling 193 defendants and a case that spanned decades—quite literally. The Old Man was a great help, particularly in organizing the facts and planning the opening arguments, but he had been out of the field so long that organizing the details wasn't his strong suit.

Neither of them wanted to bring in an assistant for the research, because the assistant wouldn't have known what was important and what wasn't.

Once Arias figured out what was important, she had a program sort all the information into her preferred format. She did use assistants, but mostly to double-check the transcriptions of the interviews done with the defendants, some by the rescuers when the *Renegat* appeared, and some by the media, before the court locked the defendants down.

There, the assistants could be helpful—and were. They found and logged hundreds of inconsistencies, and when Arias asked for those inconsistencies to be sorted by type and location, they did that as well. One assistant even flagged what she considered to be large inconsistencies and small ones.

The case had been assigned the largest courtroom in the judicial module of Starbase Sigma. The judicial wing was crammed in the very center of a tower. The uppermost and lowermost floors of the judicial module were the only parts of the tower that had any windows at all. Those windows overlooked the uglier parts of the docking ring on the lower end and the maintenance tubes for one of the more upscale areas on the upper side.

Because of the windows, though, judges had commandeered that part of the tower for office and conference room space.

The rest of the tower had no windows at all, because, the logic went, the courtrooms didn't need windows. No one wanted defendants or worse, judges, to be staring out the window instead of paying attention to whatever was going on in court.

This courtroom could seat fifty spectators. It could be modified to have twenty or more lawyers and defendants at the defense and prosecution tables.

And, of course, it had that large curved bench which seated all the judges. The curve was sharp, so that the judges on either end almost faced each other. Lawyers had to interact in the middle of that curve, so that everyone could see what was going on.

The very size of this courtroom made Arias nervous. She couldn't keep her eye on everyone here. She couldn't watch reactions and sometimes, from the prosecutor's table, she couldn't even see what was happening with the judges themselves.

She not only wanted to know if she had lost the judges with her arguments, she also wanted to know if the defense attorneys had as well.

This case was even worse, because there would be no spectators inside the court. Those fifty seats would be used by fifty defendants. They would rotate out—different defendants each day. The rest of the time, they would watch from a room in their tower, sitting as a group with some court minions keeping the group from discussing the case, as they watched their fate together.

It was a bad situation. Arias had argued that the defendants watch individually from their rooms and be recorded while doing so, but the judges in a unanimous ruling had determined that watching individually did not replicate the courtroom experience and therefore it violated some law or practice or custom.

Arias really didn't care what got violated. Once she knew her motion had been denied, she had turned her attention to other things.

The early part of this morning, her attention had been on her clothing. She needed to make sure the judges saw her, and not in a bad way. She finally chose a slate-gray suit that suggested a uniform. It had red piping and she wore comfortable red-and-gray shoes to accent the piping. No makeup, no extra color in her hair. No frills at all, because she had learned that frills made the judges take lawyers less seriously.

The Old Man wore a crisp black formal coat that went to his knees, almost like a dress. His pants matched and he had shined his shoes, something she had never seen before. His silver hair was trim, and he actually looked like he had gotten some sleep.

He had not accompanied her into the courtroom. He had arrived early as was his custom, and did some kind of private dress rehearsal in the large empty space.

It was not empty now. The defense attorney, Eun Ae Mukasey, wore an ivory tunic with gold trim over a pair of gold pants. Her shoes had platforms on the bottom and looked extremely uncomfortable. But she was one of those women who made uncomfortable shoes her own. She had her black hair pulled away from her face, accenting her features—and her clear lack of sleep.

The fifty defendants were already here as well, and were remarkably quiet. A few of them looked terrified. The rest sat at attention, as if being good listeners would count for something. Maybe it would.

All of them wore their uniforms. The design was one Arias had only seen in the historic displays during her school days. Flared pants legs, tight collars—although many had the buttons loose, because so many had gained weight. Yusef Kabac had a seat behind the defense table, and he wore his uniform jacket like a sweater. His meaty arms barely fit into it, and it was clear that the jacket would never close over his massive stomach.

At least he had trimmed his beard, and he looked like he bathed. The first time Arias had seen him, he hadn't looked clean at all.

Raina Serpell was here as well, and that couldn't have been a coincidence. She was the one who had taken point on all legal matters, just like she had been the one to captain the *Renegat* to bring them home. Arias had thought that the defendants were picked at random for their days in court, but the presence of Serpell and Kabac belied that assumption.

Not that it mattered. Arias wouldn't be speaking to them. She was going to talk to the judges. They were the only ones she had to convince of her entire case.

She wasn't nervous. She was ready, almost bouncing with too much energy. The Old Man was going to speak first. He needed to give information that she and the Old Man both assumed the judges *thought* they knew. Judges were often impatient with hearing information like that, but everyone needed to work off the same set of facts.

The Old Man was good at doing these kinds of openings, and he didn't care if the judges got angry at him. Half of them probably were anyway. After that, he would hand the bulk of the case over to Arias, and he wanted her to be as well received as possible.

So did she. She was relieved that he was starting, not because she doubted her ability to mount the same argument, but because he had a talent for making complex things sound simple.

Besides, everyone assumed this was his case; he needed to make it seem like he was the one taking point, even when he was not.

She tried very hard not to look at the door to the judges' chambers. She was ready to start.

She hoped they were too.

EIGHTEEN

Mukasey was always nervous just before a trial. She never felt like she had prepared enough, and on a case this big, she *knew* she hadn't prepared enough. There would be questions she couldn't answer, accusations she couldn't fight.

What she had to do was remain confident about her presentation. She had to remind the judges just what an unusual situation this was. Her main point? The *Renegat* Renegades had returned. They could have remained anywhere else along their journey. But they returned home.

Mutineers would not have done that.

She resisted the urge to turn around and smile at the fifty defendants who were in the room. She had already given them a pep talk as well as rules for courtroom decorum. She had broadcast those rules to the remainder of the 193 defendants, so that they wouldn't make any mistakes either.

She had been informed that the group room in their tower would be considered part of the courtroom, which why she was paying an assistant to be in the room, and to record from a different angle. She was terrified that these defendants would make some kind of mistake, something that would open a door for the prosecution.

But, as she told herself before every case, she couldn't control the people around her. She could only control herself.

And she had to do that, because this might very well be the biggest case of her life.

The judges before her were an even mix of intellectuals, long-time Fleet officers, and former lawyers. The chief judge for this case, Marcus Kanberra, had sat in the center chair on one of her earlier cases. He had gone out of his way to be fair, which was exactly what she needed in this case.

She tugged at her tunic, then fiddled with the bracelet she wore on her left wrist. She had worn that bracelet on every case she had ever tried, and usually the feel of it against her skin kept her calm. Not this time.

Nothing was going to keep her calm. She was going to have to flow with the nervous energy and use it to her advantage.

She shot a glance at the prosecution table. They looked as understaffed as she was, although she knew that wasn't true. They had associates who had done some of the legwork. She had run into them.

She had a bit of help, most of it from interns and law students who wanted extra hours. She had brought in a few associates, but only on tasks that she felt they couldn't screw up.

Chief Judge Kanberra gaveled the court to order, and launched into his usual spiel about courtroom behavior, procedures, lunch breaks and other administration items. Mukasey paid attention only because she knew he would add a few details to deal with the unbelievable number of defendants.

But he had given the courtroom instructions to both sides to approve or reject two days ago, and neither side had any complaints. So she listened only to make certain he hadn't left out anything or added anything without her realizing it.

The instructions took twenty minutes. By then, Judge Chiara Ioannide, who was one of the newest judges on the bench, seemed to be nodding off. Her colleague, Ati Velsia, elbowed her. Ioannide started.

That wasn't a good way to start the case, with at least one judge already bored with the proceedings. As if on cue, Chief Judge Kanberra turned to the prosecution table.

"Are you ready to begin?" he asked.

"We are, sir." The Old Man stood. Apparently he didn't need more of an invitation.

Mukasey leaned back in her chair, holding a tablet in one hand for notes. She had never seen the Old Man work although she had heard he was brilliant.

He didn't start that way.

"Your Honors," he said, "I know we have all followed the media reports of the miraculous return of the *Renegat*, through dozens of fold-space trips, much hardship, an attack when they stopped for food, and a mission that had gone awry. However, we all got the story piecemeal, so I would like to make sure we are working off the same set of facts."

Ioannide shook her head once, as if she couldn't believe this was how the case was going to start.

At least two judges, Théodolphe Bastien and Dev Jatrana, looked pointedly at Mukasey, expecting her to object. She saw no point in doing so. The Old Man was right; they needed to start with the same set of facts. She would contradict some of them—or testimony would—but fighting at this stage made very little difference.

The Old Man was a good storyteller. He started with the arrival of the *Renegat* as the Fleet was shutting down Sector Base Z. Had they arrived a few days later, no one would have rescued the ship. The defendants would have died not too far from their destination.

After telling that part—the rescue, the loss of some of the crew members and a heroic member of the *Aizsargs* who refused to give up—the Old Man asked if he could be a bit more informal and sit on his table.

Chief Judge Kanberra let him. The Old Man actually leaned on the table sideways, so that he could see the defense table, the judges, and most of the defendants.

If Mukasey had no knowledge of the case, she would have thought that he was the defense attorney. He sounded sympathetic to the *Renegat* crew. He believed that the distance they had traveled against all odds, the fact that they had made it home only to find that home no longer existed, made them capture the hearts of anyone who had been following the news of the *Renegat*.

"The facts that are in dispute," he said, "are not the ones I just recited. What happened on the *Renegat's* long journey and how this group of 193 people returned home, instead of the remainder of the nearly five hundred who had left on that fateful mission are what we need to determine here. Because we will prove that the defendants are not heroes. They are mutineers who, among other things, murdered the ship's captain and abandoned their mission. Their return was not because they wanted to return to the Fleet, but because they were so incompetent they did not know how to go anywhere else. They fought and were terrified of each other. It was nearly impossible for them to act as a group, so they fled back to what they knew, hoping that they would receive sympathy for their journey and no one would notice the price others paid for the return of the *Renegat*."

She could have objected. In fact, a few of the judges clearly expected her to. But she didn't.

He had the right to propose his theory of the case, even if it sounded strangely weak and vague. From what she knew about the Old Man, he was never weak or vague, not in his arguments. Either he was hiding something, or they really didn't care about this early information.

"The *Renegat* left the Fleet on an unusual mission," the Old Man said, "one that took them in a direction the Fleet rarely goes—backwards. They were to investigate information that came from an ancient Scrapheap. Someone had marauded it—years ago. But they were to determine if the marauders took anything of value, meaning the Ready Vessels, and if the marauders had, then the Fleet had to decide what to do about it."

Mukasey clutched her tablet tightly. That was one way to describe the mission.

"But the *Renegat* never fulfilled its mission. Instead, there was chaos and confusion from the start. They did reach the Scrapheap, and returned home almost immediately thereafter, having determined nothing." The Old Man looked at the defendants as if he had nothing but contempt for them.

A few looked away, even though Mukasey had told them to maintain eye contact at all times.

"The media reports don't talk about the fact that every aspect of the

Renegat's mission was a failure, from the internal conflicts to their inability to complete the mission to the loss of the ship upon return. Not to mention an inexplicable loss of hundreds of crew members. What, exactly, happened to all of them?"

The Old Man continued to look at the defendants, as if he expected them to answer. More heads went down. But Raina Serpell continued to meet his gaze.

Serpell almost looked defiant. Maybe Mukasey had been wrong in her advice. Maybe they should have been a bit more humble.

"Heroes, misfits, incompetents." The Old Man directed each word at the defendants. "Such nice descriptions of mutineers and murderers."

More judges looked at Mukasey. But she didn't interrupt his rhythm. Let him have his say. She would have hers shortly.

"The so-called *Renegat* Renegades are famous throughout the Fleet." The Old Man stood up. "That is why we need to expose the truth of what they've done and punish them for it. All of our ships travel to parts unknown, often by themselves. The ships have to function well. The chain of command must remain unbroken, even in the face of commands that the rank and file do not like or understand. The only way the Fleet can function is with crews that work together toward a common goal."

The Old Man walked up to the bench, and made a point of looking at the judges. Mukasey always felt awkward when she did that.

"Yeah, they went through hell," the Old Man said, punctuating each sentence with a look at a different judge. "They were on a difficult mission with a difficult captain. Many of us have gone through hell as well. Many of us had disagreements with our leaders. We did not kill them and run home, expecting to lie our way to retirement. Some wag in the media suggested that these *Renegat* survivors are the very best of us."

The Old Man let out a slight chuckle.

"Their propaganda is working. Because they are anything but the best of us. They are the worst of us, and they must be made an example of."

Then he bowed his head, thanked the judges for their time, and returned to his seat. Lucinda Arias didn't pat him on the shoulder or even smile at him. She had her head bent as she went to work.

During this speech, though, no judge had looked away. Even Ioannide now seemed wide awake and interested.

Mukasey's stomach knotted. She knew only one solution to her nerves.

She stood up, and formally introduced herself to the court, just like the Old Man had done at the beginning of his opening statement.

Then she said, "Your Honors, we're not here to label anyone. Mr. Yglesias seems to think we care about what the media calls my clients. We don't care about labels. My clients are by definition defendants in this case, and they are survivors of a horrific journey. They managed to return to the Fleet against all odds, and now Mr. Yglesias wants to punish them for that."

She slid around the desk and walked toward the bench. Her platform shoes made her taller, so that she could see each judge clearly. She could also see which judges were tapping notes into their tablets and which had their hands folded as they listened to the arguments.

"This mission was doomed from the start. The evidence will show that the Fleet felt an obligation to investigate that ancient Scrapheap, but doubted that investigation would be worthwhile. So they outfitted a Security-Class vessel, which was not designed for that kind of travel, filled it with crew members who had no family and no real reputation—the kind of people who would not be missed if they disappeared or died—and sent them the longest distance a Fleet ship has ever traveled on its own."

The judges were watching her closely. She couldn't remember a time when she'd ever had the attention of all twelve judges in a tribunal.

"Unbeknownst to the crew, this ship was not supposed to come back. It was supposed to go to the Scrapheap, discover what had happened, and send that information back. What happened to the ship and her crew afterwards was irrelevant."

She paused for effect.

"Most of you have worked in command," she said quietly. "You know that ships sometimes get sent on a mission like this, one they're not expected to survive. Those ships are usually well-equipped and properly staffed. This ship was on a mission no one thought could succeed, but the rules stated that incursions into Scrapheaps needed to be investigated. So, they sent this single ship, unprepared and poorly maintained, to investigate. A lot went wrong, and, as you will see, most of it could have been both predicted and prevented."

She looked at the defendants. They were all watching her now, most rigidly holding still, so that they could hide the emotions they were feeling, but a few looking both sad and terrified, and a handful seeming surprised.

"The most unexpected thing," she said as she turned back to the judges, "was how terrifyingly bad at his job Captain Preemas was. And this entire ship, poorly prepared and improperly staffed, had no recourse. They were on their own in ways that no ship of the Fleet ever should be. They were ill served, and yet they still did their best."

Then she paused again for effect, aware that she was not the orator that the Old Man was. Still, she had the judges' attention.

"They didn't come back because they were incompetent. They didn't come back to lie to the Fleet. They came back because the Fleet is their home. They struggled against incredible odds, and they managed to return, just like they were supposed to."

Judge Jatrana nodded, then caught himself. Mukasey didn't want to take that as a hopeful sign, but she did anyway.

She moved a little closer to the bench.

"I'm not suggesting they're heroes," Mukasey said. "I'm simply saying this: If they had believed they had done something wrong, they could have remained in that Scrapheap with the rest of the crew."

She took a well-timed breath, so that it didn't quite sound like a dramatic pause. But she wanted that bit of information to go in. She would repeat it a lot, but the first time was always the most important.

"Or," she said, "they could have stopped anywhere along the way. There were old Fleet sector bases at some of the *Renegat's* foldspace checkpoints. The crew would have been able to find places to live or even ships to work on. They didn't choose that. They chose to come here, hoping they'd arrive ninety-nine years in our past, one year in their future. It didn't turn out that way."

She let the sadness she felt about that show on her face.

"These are not master criminals or selfish people. They're people who did their best in an unprecedented situation. They should not be jailed for what they've done. They should be repatriated. They should be helped into this future they find themselves in. They should be welcomed home."

She nodded, just like the Old Man had, and returned to her seat. Her body was shaking ever so slightly, and she was having trouble catching her breath.

She had done it, and she had done well enough against the Old Man.

Now the real work of the trial began. The evidence, the organization, the massive job of keeping the prosecution off-course.

She was ready for that. She did better with that than with all other aspects of being in court.

She was going to give this trial her all. She had to. All 193 people depended on her—and she didn't want to disappoint a single one of them.

NINETEEN

The initial presentation of the case went faster than Arias expected. Maybe her expectations had been shaped by the sheer number of defendants, or maybe it was the mass of information, but either way, she had thought it would take a lot longer to get through some of this material.

One thing that didn't conform to her expectations were the judges. In previous cases, the judges had always asked too many questions. They had interrupted the flow or taken the questioning in a different direction.

In previous trials, she had had judges completely derail some of her witnesses or disqualify them after a few questions.

That hadn't happened here. There also hadn't been a lot of objections where she thought there would be.

She had established the history of the Scrapheap, the fact that it was so far distant from where the Fleet was now that there had been no records of it before it notified the Fleet of a breach. She showed the chain of command, used records to prove that Preemas had been chosen as captain over several other candidates, and also entered into the record all 193 agreements that the defendants had sworn to before embarking on the *Renegat.*

She hadn't even bothered to read any of those records aloud because everyone in this courtroom—except maybe Mukasey—had attested to those kinds of agreements before accepting their postings. It was standard, and what Arias wanted to prove by using those agreements was that this trip, despite its strange destination, was handled just like any other journey by any other ship of the Fleet.

Then she and the Old Man showed the dramatic footage of the *Renegat's* rescue. They had edited the images because the rescue had taken place over hours, and they didn't have hours. So they showed the highlights, from different angles than those usually shown in the media. She also had footage of the final life raft, leaving the *Renegat* with the last few survivors on board as well as Raul Zarges who had defied orders to save his own life to take the remaining survivors on the last life raft.

The *Renegat* had been cleared, the life raft had floated away from it—and then the heartbreaking explosion, the loss of the *Renegat* and the last few survivors and Raul Zarges, whom his entire crew loved.

Arias and the Old Man had fought over including that footage, and she had won. She felt she needed it. Members of the *Aizsargs* were going to testify about the crew of the *Renegat,* and before they did, she had to make sure the judges—and everyone else following this show trial—knew that the *Aizsargs* had put everything on the line to save the crew of the *Renegat.*

The *Aizsargs* had been called back to Starbase Sigma just so several members of the crew could testify. Arias would call others to establish that the materials from the *Renegat's* bridge were downloaded onto the *Aizsargs* and were complete. She would have some of the rescuers discuss what they had found in that dark and nearly destroyed ship.

But first, she called Captain Kim Dauber of the *Aizsargs* to testify.

The witness box in this courtroom was in the very center of the half circle. The box rose when needed, and sank when it wasn't in use. The witnesses faced the judges, not the gallery, but the gallery could see the images of the witnesses in real time displayed on the back of the witness chair.

Because of the placement of the defense and prosecution tables, anyone seated could see both the display and the witness. Arias always made sure she stood during testimony so that she could see the actual witness and not the display. Sometimes, she lost little bits of information —micro expressions or a subtle hand gesture—on the display.

Before trials even started, she asked for permission to stand at the end of the table, next to the most junior judge, so that she could watch everything.

The judges didn't care where she stood as long as she didn't make noise when someone else was examining or cross-examining the witness.

She also could not give small signals to her own witnesses under cross-examination. Not that she would ever have done that.

The Old Man didn't care about perspective. He remained at the prosecution table when the clerk of the court called Captain Dauber to the witness stand.

Those small moments in court always had a lot of ceremony—the witness called, the witness box either rising or tuning to the new occupant, that moment when the gallery would turn, sometimes as a unit, to see who the new witness was.

In this case, the entire gallery—all fifty of them—knew Captain Dauber. She had been the unlucky soul to inform them that they were one hundred years in their future. That couldn't be a good memory for any of them, even though they had survived against all odds.

Of course, it had been more than a year since they had seen Captain Dauber, and a lot had happened in between. They also met Dauber in the middle of a rescue, not the crisp and trim woman who had arrived in court.

She wore her dress uniform, hat tucked under one arm, her black hair stiff and styled against her skull. Every part of her looked in control.

She walked with perfect military bearing to the witness chair, where she had sat many times before. She set her hat on her knee, went through the formalities which included her name, her service history, and a reminder that her position required her to tell the truth.

She answered each question, which had come from the clerk not Arias, firmly and precisely. Dauber spoke clearly. The judges didn't have to lean in to hear her.

Arias took Dauber through the rescue, drawing out personal details, such as the entire bridge crew's shock at the type of vessel they were seeing, how they handled the realization that the ship was not an upgraded SC-class vessel, but an older one, and one that they didn't immediately have records on.

Arias didn't linger on the process the *Aizsargs* had used to identify the *Renegat*, although it fascinated her every time she heard it.

Instead, she focused on the loss of personnel, dealing with the disoriented survivors, and the conversations that Dauber had with them as they headed toward Starbase Sigma.

Finally, Arias got to the heart of the testimony.

"You're the one who recommended that the crew of the *Renegat* be charged with mutiny, am I right?"

She knew she wasn't right, but she wanted this on record in a specific way. She had explained that to Dauber when they discussed the testimony.

"No," Dauber said. "I did not recommend any charges at all. I had asked for an investigation of the *Renegat's* crew."

There. Now, it would be harder for Mukasey to say that Dauber had an agenda, that Dauber *wanted* to go after the *Renegat's* crew because they had cost her a valued member of her own crew.

"Isn't an investigation standard procedure when a ship blows up?" Arias asked.

"Yes," Dauber said, "which is why we worked so hard to save the crew and the ship's records."

"You saved all but six of the crew," Arias said, "in tight circumstances without any warning."

"Yes." Dauber's voice had grown soft. Arias knew that the loss of the six was a sore point for Dauber, almost as sore as losing Raul Zarges.

"Were you able to save any information?" she asked.

"We pulled all the information we could find from the *Renegat*'s systems. We have procedures for that, and we did the best we could."

"There are gaps in the information pulled from the *Renegat*," Arias said.

"Not from our efforts," Dauber said. "Those gaps are in the *Renegat's* files."

"You saw that from the beginning?" Arias asked.

"We knew that some of the ship's recent history had been scrubbed," Dauber said.

"Is that why you asked for a broader investigation?" Arias asked.

"I didn't ask for a broader investigation," Dauber said. "I recommended a very specific investigation. I wanted an investigation into the relationships of the crew. Most specifically, I wanted to know how a linguist ended up in charge of a security-class vessel on a very important mission."

"You're referring to Raina Serpell?" Arias asked. Serpell was not in the court on this day, so Arias couldn't see her face. Arias had a hunch that Serpell did not know until this moment that Dauber hadn't trusted her.

Arias had asked the associate who was monitoring the defendants in the other location to keep a close eye on them during this testimony. It was the beginning of a lot of crucial statements. This was where the actual case against the *Renegat* Renegades began.

"Yes, I'm referring to Raina Serpell," Dauber said. "She identified herself as the person in charge. So did Yusef Kabac, but no one else corroborated that."

"Kabac the engineer," Arias said.

"He had been demoted as an engineer by Nadim Crowe when he was chief engineer," Dauber said. "However, on the journey back, Kabac was the only remaining engineer on the ship."

"The *only* remaining engineer?" Arias asked. "What did you think when you learned that?"

"I was stunned," Dauber said. "I had no idea how a ship could lose all of its engineers."

"And that aroused your suspicion?" Arias asked.

"That, and the fact that *all* of the senior staff was no longer on the ship. Not just Captain Preemas, who was killed, but anyone who could logically take his place." Dauber's hand touched the hat on her lap. That movement was the only sign of distress that she showed.

Arias knew, from their previous discussions, that the absence of the *Renegat's* senior staff didn't just strike Dauber as unusual. It worried her greatly.

"There had been a battle for control of the ship," Arias said. "We will get to some of the details of that later. Did you know about the battle at the time?"

"Vaguely," Dauber said.

"So you might have assumed that the senior staff was no longer on the ship after that rebellion against Captain Preemas." Arias was not going to use the word "mutiny" again while questioning Dauber. Not yet, anyway.

"I don't assume anything," Dauber said. "We are a rescue vehicle. We gather information and give it to the Fleet. What we learn has to be as thorough as possible, because sometimes our efforts are the only ones possible. That's what happened with the *Renegat.* We pulled the records, and then the ship blew up."

"Do you know the cause of the explosion?" Arias asked.

"I don't, no, not exactly," Dauber said. "It seemed to be a problem with the *anacapa* drive. There was nothing my people could do to stop the explosion in the time we had."

"You tried?" Arias asked.

Dauber looked pained. "We always try. Sometimes we can solve problems. Here we could not."

Arias took a breath, letting that sink in. Then she said, "This ship clearly went through a lot. It seems logical that they would lose people along the way, particularly considering all they saw. What made you think this was different?"

Dauber's fingers moved on the side of her hat, just slightly, but enough to show the anger that wasn't on her face. She was furious about the loss of the senior staff, and the way that the *Renegat* Renegades behaved in the aftermath of their arrival. The *Renegat* Renegades gave interviews, and they went through the protocols as if they expected to be lauded for returning, not for any behavior they performed on the mission itself.

"The type of people lost," Dauber said. "We learned that Preemas had shifted his crew around to different positions, so someone might have started as bridge crew but became a chef, to cite just one example. That meant there were a lot of experienced people on that ship, not just in obvious positions, like bridge crew or engineering, but in other positions as well. *None* of those people made it back here. Not a single one."

Her fingers gripped the edge of her hat. Her voice held just a bit of the controlled fury that Arias knew was inside her.

"Perhaps," Arias said, anticipating Mukasey's questions, "the difficulties went across various departments in the ship, so it took out the people who were in charge."

Dauber shook her head. "I checked before I talked with Raina Serpell the very last time," she said. "There was a skirmish on the way back, but the only person who died was Serpell's wife India Romano. Everyone else survived."

Dauber made that point as if it were important. Arias hadn't thought about that before. Serpell's wife died as well? And their marriage had been in trouble, because Romano had joined the *Renegat* by misleading Serpell to join her. By the time Serpell had realized that, she'd had to follow, to keep the marriage alive.

Arias made a mental note of that, not sure what she would do with it. Maybe if Mukasey was foolish enough to put Serpell in the witness chair, then Arias would press that point.

But before she could move to the next point, Judge Ati Velsia leaned forward. She was an older woman with dark intelligent eyes, and a take-no-prisoners manner. She had been paying close attention to every detail of this case, unlike a few of her colleagues.

"You make that point about the wife, Romano, as if we should read something into it, Captain," Judge Velsia said. "Do you want us to?"

Arias took a quiet deep breath to keep herself calm. She did not look at the Old Man, although she wanted to. She didn't want this case to go sideways. It was too important and it had too many pieces.

"The death of Serpell's wife disturbs me, Your Honor," Dauber said. "There were reports from the other crew members that Serpell and her wife no longer got along, and a few suggested to me that there was a power struggle between the two of them over the way that Serpell was running the ship."

"Do you have proof of this?" Judge Dev Jatrana asked. He had continually glanced from Mukasey to Arias, those glances looked not just empathetic, but like silent commands: *Are you going to object? Did you notice what the prosecution is doing here?*

"Please clarify for me, Your Honor," Dauber said with the aplomb of someone who had been through this kind of situation many times. "Which part are you concerned about?"

"That Serpell and Romano fought for control of the ship?" Judge Jatrana asked.

"Your Honor, I have the testimony of others, given to me as we brought the survivors to Starbase Sigma. That kind of information is often used in court in lieu of evidence, especially when a ship has been destroyed."

"I'm aware of the law," Judge Jatrana said stiffly, as if she had offended him.

Arias was glad that she didn't have to remind him that there were permutations to witness testimony, particularly in the case of a destroyed ship.

Jatrana leaned back, signaling the end to his questioning.

Arias waited half a beat before continuing.

"So," Arias said as she brought the case back on track, "only one person died after the *Renegat* left the Scrapheap."

"Yes," Dauber said.

"The loss of the senior staff occurred at the Scrapheap, is that correct?" Arias asked.

"At or near it," Dauber said.

"At the same time as the death of Captain Preemas?" Arias asked.

"Objection." Mukasey stood. "Captain Dauber was not on the ship. She would have no knowledge of this."

"Captain, where does your knowledge come from?" Chief Judge Kanberra asked. There was a tone in his voice: he was annoyed at the objection.

"I studied the logs, sir, and the death records, and I interviewed the survivors," Dauber said in that same just-the-facts voice she'd been using.

"You may proceed," Chief Judge Kanberra said.

Mukasey sat down slowly, as if she hadn't liked his answer.

"There was a lot of loss about the same time as the death of Captain Preemas," Dauber said. "The media ended up calling that moment the 'Battle for the *Renegat*,' and I think that might be apt. As in any battle, a number of people died."

"But not all of the people you've mentioned, is that correct?" Arias asked.

"Most of the senior staff survived the battle for the *Renegat*," Dauber said. "According to some of the statements I got, the senior staff left the *Renegat* voluntarily to remain at the Scrapheap."

"And what did the other statements say?" Arias asked.

"That they had no idea why the senior staff left," Dauber said.

"You pulled records off the ship. Do the records show that the senior staff wanted to stay behind at the Scrapheap?" Arias asked.

"No." Dauber let the word hang, just like Arias had initially wanted her to.

There was a stirring in the courtroom, mostly among the judges. Arias did not look. She kept her gaze on Dauber.

"What do the records show?" Arias asked.

"Nothing," Dauber said. "They've been scrubbed."

"Scrubbed? Not erased in the crisis?" Arias asked.

"Scrubbed," Dauber said.

"I object," Mukasey said. "There's no way that a ship's captain can know that."

"Most ship captains do not know the situation on other ships," Arias said. She had been expecting that objection. "But Captain Dauber's remit, on a DV-Class vessel tasked with rescuing other ships and helping close down sectors, gives her an expertise in handling strange computer systems. She has learned how to recognize when information was deleted due to circumstances, such as a faulty system that could lead to ship failure, or when information was deleted by a human actor."

"Is that so, Captain Dauber?" Chief Judge Kanberra asked.

"Yes, Your Honor. Human error can sometimes be repaired quickly. Faulty systems take more work." Dauber had folded her hands behind her hat. She was calmer now.

"You said 'human error,'" Chief Judge Kanberra said. "Is that what you think the deletion of the information on the *Renegat* was?"

"I do not think that the deletion of information was human error," Dauber said. "I believe it was deliberate."

"What leads you to that conclusion?" Chief Judge Kanberra asked.

"The scrubbing took place over many days and in many systems. It only covered the time period after the *Renegat* reached the Scrapheap until shortly after the *Renegat's* departure. The scrubbing was done either by someone incompetent or someone who did not know how to scrub properly. There should have been echoes of the information throughout the backup systems."

"Should have been, Captain?" Chief Judge Kanberra asked.

Arias kept her expression neutral. She had worried about bringing this information in. It was speculative, and usually judges didn't like that.

But she hadn't brought it forward. The Chief Judge himself had done so, and without thinking about the nature of the evidence.

Or perhaps he had thought of it. Chief Judge Kanberra was a canny man. If he continued to play the case this way, then she would know what side of the case he leaned to. Right now, it seemed like he leaned toward her.

She didn't dare get cocky about it, though.

"Yes, Your Honor, 'should have been,'" Dauber said. "We were only able to download the primary systems in the time we had. We were not able to touch all of the backups. Normally, we would have investigated material off of them, and we would have found the echoes, given the kind of scrubbing that was done."

"Is there nowhere else these backup files would be?" Chief Judge Kanberra asked.

Arias felt a small thread of surprise. She would not have thought to ask that question.

"Normally, Your Honor, there might have been backups on nearby ships, since sometimes, especially in extremis, ships are programmed to send their files to nearby Fleet ships to avoid a complete loss. But the *Renegat* had arrived directly from foldspace, and to my knowledge, had had no contact with any other ship from the Fleet during that time."

"Except your ship," Chief Judge Kanberra said.

"We looked," Captain Dauber asked. "There was no automated backup done in the time we were near the *Renegat*."

"Isn't that a failure on your part?" Chief Judge Kanberra asked.

Arias winced internally. So maybe that was where he was going, blaming the Captain.

"No, Your Honor," Captain Dauber said. She did not seem at all perturbed by Chief Judge Kanberra's question. Maybe she had encountered questions like this before. Or maybe she knew what the judge was about. "The backup is always enabled by the failing ship. It's part of any ship of the Fleet's emergency protocol."

"Even a ship as old as the *Renegat*?" Chief Judge Kanberra asked.

"Yes," Dauber said. "I checked when we had no backup copy. This backup method has been a part of the Fleet for at least a couple of centuries, maybe longer."

She couldn't be more specific than a couple of centuries because the Fleet didn't always keep track of history like that. Arias mentally applauded Dauber. She was doing even better than Arias had hoped she would.

"Was that automated backup system deliberately taken offline?" Chief Judge Kanberra asked.

"I don't know, Your Honor," Dauber said. "I'm not sure there is a way to know. My guess is no, it was not deliberate. Given the way the information was scrubbed, I don't believe that anyone in the remaining crew of the *Renegat* knew about these redundant systems."

Chief Judge Kanberra frowned at her, as if he didn't like that answer.

Apparently, Dauber noticed it and risked one more thought.

"To be frank, Your Honor—" she said, with enough time between the phrase and whatever she was going to say next to allow him to interrupt. He did not. "—the *Renegat* was in terrible shape when we found her. Many of her systems had failed. I think it's logical to assume that many of the backup protocols were offline for many systems, and that some of them had been offline for some time."

"In your opinion," Chief Judge Kanberra said, "that is because the *Renegat* no longer had engineers?"

Had Arias asked that question, Mukasey would have objected. But the chief judge had asked. Mukasey had to be careful about how she was going to handle her response to this line of questioning.

"The defendants had almost no experience with the practical methods of running a ship," Dauber said. "I found evidence in the data that the *help* systems and the autopilot systems were accessed many times, mostly as a teaching tool."

Three of the judges lowered their heads, not in disgust, but to hide expressions of amazement.

Amazement. Arias understood that reaction. It was amazing that the

Renegat had returned, given how many problems it had faced—not just the mutiny or the loss of the senior staff, but an attack on the way back and a completely incompetent crew.

"Did those help systems tell them how to scrub data?" Chief Judge Kanberra asked.

"I don't know," Dauber said. "It's not in modern help files. It's not something we ever want crews to do."

The logic of that seemed to catch several of the judges. They nodded, even though they weren't supposed to react to evidence.

"There is one other thing, Your Honor," Dauber said. Arias's breath caught. She had no idea what Dauber was going to say, and that made her nervous.

Chief Judge Kanberra glanced at Arias, as if he wondered whether he'd been set up.

She let some of the nerves cross her face.

That seemed to make a decision for him. "All right," he said. "What is this one more thing?"

"There are no bridge records from the *Renegat* after the battle that occurred near the planet Amnthra. None. Someone shut off all of the systems that recorded every move crew members made, the orders that were given, and everything the ship encountered."

Arias had planned to introduce that information later, when she tried to cram the information about the scrubbing. She had planned to bring that up after Mukasey's cross-examination of Dauber.

The fact that it came up now meant Arias would have to change her strategy a bit, but she could do that.

"No records," Chief Judge Kanberra repeated. "Because they were scrubbed?"

"Some of the records around the time of the battle were scrubbed," Dauber said. "Shortly after the battle, though, the system had been deliberately taken offline."

"So you're telling me that two different incidents that the *Renegat* was involved inspired someone to scrub the records?"

"Yes, Your Honor," Dauber said.

"And then deliberately shut down another system?" he asked, sounding surprised.

"Yes, Your Honor," Dauber said.

"How do you know this was deliberate?" he asked.

"Because, Your Honor," she said, "we have the records. The system is designed to let us know why it isn't functioning."

"Huh," Chief Judge Kanberra said, as if he didn't know what to do with that information. His gaze met Arias's.

"I think I've dominated the questioning long enough," he said to her. "Take us back to the questions you needed to ask."

"Thank you, Your Honor," Arias said.

She felt a bit off balance. Part of her mind started working on how to reintroduce that information. But she also had to mentally delete several other questions, since the answers he had pulled out of Dauber had answered those questions sideways anyhow.

Arias walked from one side of the witness chair to the other, not for any reason except to reassert dominance, remind everyone that this was her questioning now.

"Captain Dauber," Arias said. "You recommended that this starbase investigate the crew of the *Renegat*."

"Yes," Dauber said.

"Let me be sure I have this right." Arias had launched into the practiced part of the testimony. "You recommended it because you learned about Captain Preemas."

"Yes," Dauber said.

"The entire senior staff had left the ship so far from the Fleet that they might never be able to return." Arias knew that she was asserting information not in evidence yet, but if no one challenged this, then she never had to.

"Yes," Dauber said.

"And," Arias said, "the evidence of what happened at that Scrapheap had been scrubbed inexpertly from the system."

"Yes," Dauber said, "and from the period around the battle near Amnthra."

Good for her, bringing that back around.

"Aside from the things you listed," Arias said, "is there anything else that made you recommend the investigation of the *Renegat*?"

"Yes," Dauber said, which made Arias's heart beat just a bit faster even though she had known that was how Dauber would answer. "I simply did not trust anyone I met from the *Renegat*."

Arias waited half a beat, expecting Mukasey to object. But Mukasey was apparently smart enough to realize that Dauber's opinion was not something she could object to, not before tribunal. Maybe if they had used civilians, which the Fleet rarely did.

"That seems very subjective to me," Arias said. If Mukasey wasn't going to make the argument, then Arias would do so.

"It's not," Dauber said. "There are two reasons why I didn't trust any of them. The first comes from the fact that when I asked what happened to the senior staff, I got two answers, and only two. From 193 people. Based on interviews I've done in past crises, I should have received dozens of different answers from different perspectives."

Arias did not ask the follow-up question, *Do you think they were coached?*, because she knew that Mukasey would object to that. Arias had to trust that the judges understood Dauber's point.

"The other reason?" Arias asked.

"The other reason, and the reason I finally decided to make my recommendations, was the interview I had done with Raina Serpell."

Arias turned to the bench. "Your Honors, we have the interview ready to play. I would like to enter all of it into evidence, with a flag on the portion we are going to play."

"So ordered," Chief Judge Kanberra said.

Arias nodded at the Old Man. He held one of their tablets. He handed it to her. She set it on the arm of the witness chair.

"May I?" Dauber asked.

Arias barely managed not to give her a look of surprise. Dauber had something planned, and Arias could either shut it down—and maybe discredit her own witness—or she could let it play out.

Dauber had been through as many or more trials than Arias had. Arias had to trust her.

"Certainly," Arias said, and tilted the tablet toward her.

Dauber activated the holo.

The holo had been recorded in a meeting room on the *Aizsargs*. Arias used Dauber to set up the location and the date of the interview.

Much of the room was not in the holo. The recordings were done so that the only thing that appeared with clarity was the table where Serpell and Dauber sat.

That table was small, and looked like it was on the ground in the courtroom, rather than part of a holo. A thinner Raina Serpell with stress lines on her face sat at the table, some pastries to her right, and a mug of steaming tea to her left.

It looked like she had touched neither.

Dauber fast-forwarded the recording until she found a spot slightly before the spot that Arias had flagged.

Somewhere during the recording, Dauber had shown up, sat down, and proceeded to talk with Serpell. They were discussing something and gesturing at each other.

The Dauber in the holo was not wearing her dress uniform. Her hair was slightly mussed and she looked exhausted. This was shortly after the rescue, and the hard work that Dauber had been doing showed in her face, but not in her posture. It was as rigid as it was on the stand.

Dauber finally found the moment she'd been searching for. The holo stopped fast forwarding, as the holo-Dauber was talking.

"We got as much of the Renegat*'s records as we could," holo-Dauber said. "At first, we were looking for* anacapa *anomalies, but we're finding a lot of other questions."*

Holo-Serpell swallowed visibly. Her eyes widened as if the question shocked her.

"We got a lot of material, but the bridge records disappear at the most crucial time," holo-Dauber said. "They stopped just as the Renegat *was heading to that planet that your system identified as Amnthra. What happened?"*

Arias tried not to step back. So this was what Dauber wanted to show. The lead into the snippet that Arias had planned. Arias had planned to play the lie, but Dauber wanted the setup.

Apparently she didn't think the lie would be enough for this panel.

Arias had to trust her.

Holo-Serpell squirmed, literally. It was clear that the simple question made her very uncomfortable.

"Um," holo-Serpell said, "they were probably destroyed during the battle. We took a lot of hits."

Holo-Dauber shook her head slightly, clearly not believing Serpell.

"Fleet ships are designed with a lot of redundant systems, particularly when it comes to keeping track of what happens to the ship herself," holo-Dauber said. "I'm sure we'll find other information but what we have at the moment suggests that someone went back and erased all of the information from that battle forward. Why would anyone do that?"

Holo-Serpell continued to squirm.

"What happened?" holo-Dauber asked again.

Holo-Serpell blinked hard, as if she considered crying, and was stopping herself. Her hands shook, and so did her voice as she started to speak.

"It was just really hard. I…listened to the crew. They wanted more supplies, and we shouldn't have done that. Once the weapons on that planet started firing on us, I hit every single control panel I could think of to defend us. None of us knew how the weapons' system worked or what to do with the shields. So I poked around and got lucky. I probably deleted the records or did something wrong right then."

Arias shut the holo right there. The images froze. She wanted the two of them to remain in that slightly antagonistic tableau, just for drama's sake.

She had planned on showing only that part where Serpell had blamed the crew for her own errors, and then the lie about the "accidental" deletion.

But Dauber had been right. The entire excerpt was better.

"What bothered you about this exchange?" Arias asked.

"It's all a lie," Dauber said.

"Objection," Mukasey said, as she stood. "Captain Dauber was not on the ship at that time. There is no way she could know what the truth was."

Chief Judge Kanberra looked tired. He had once served on ships, and Mukasey had not. That made a big difference.

"Overruled," he said. "Continue, Captain."

Only it was Arias who spoke next.

"How do you know it was a lie?" she asked.

"Because there is no way that someone 'poking around' could accidentally scrub the bridge records *while* they were activating weapons and shields. The systems aren't just different, they are housed in a different part of the ship."

"Even on an SC-Class vessel that old?" Arias asked.

"Especially on a vessel that old," Dauber said. "The systems that kept track of everything the ship was doing were housed on a different level, with separate controls."

"So whoever shut these down," Arias said, "had to know that."

"Yes," Dauber said.

Arias shut down the holo. The table, the steaming mug, the two women who looked like they were about to come to blows, vanished.

"Thank you," Arias said.

She returned to her seat, still feeling a little unbalanced. She wasn't quite sure how that went.

Mukasey stood up. She looked slightly angry, as if the rulings against her had set her off.

"Isn't it possible that Raina Serpell believed she had shut down those systems when she was 'poking' around?" Mukasey asked.

"Her body language suggests otherwise," Dauber said.

Arias folded her hands on the desk, focusing on them so that she wouldn't smile at Dauber's answer.

"But isn't it possible?" Mukasey asked.

"Someone knew," Dauber said.

"But maybe not Serpell," Mukasey said.

She was testifying now, but Arias would let it hang. Apparently, the Old Man agreed with her, because he didn't object either.

"I suppose there's a slight chance of that," Dauber said.

"Which would make what she said to you not a lie, right?" Mukasey said.

"I have received a lot of training in interview techniques," Dauber said. "In that interview, she repeatedly lied to me."

"But maybe not about the loss of data," Mukasey said.

"I think you would have to ask her," Dauber said.

She clearly wasn't going to budge. Mukasey glared at her, knowing that she had lost this exchange.

"Thank you," Mukasey said and walked toward her seat.

Arias had expected her to continue to press about the lies, about the subjectivity of the word "trust." Arias probably would have.

Although, Mukasey was a good and cautious lawyer. She knew she would have to fight this witness, whom the chief judge believed, and Mukasey clearly believed that would work against her.

"I have nothing more," Mukasey said.

"Redirect?" Chief Judge Kanberra said.

"I'd like to reserve the redirect," Arias said. There was more to that holo, and she might just use it if she needed it.

"Then we are adjourned for the day," Chief Judge Kanberra asked, and gaveled the session closed.

TWENTY

Long day. Arias and the Old Man returned to the office. It was dark, but that didn't mean anything. Sometimes, an attorney shut off the lights just before settling on the couch.

Arias grabbed an extra tablet. Hers was starting to fritz. But she didn't want to fix it until she had moved the rest of her case notes, holos, and information onto something new.

At this stage in a trial, she was paranoid. She didn't want anyone else to see what she was doing, and she was afraid that the defense might send someone to steal a tablet and call the theft an accident.

Someone had hacked into the prosecution's automated backups during one of her first major trials. The defense had always claimed they hadn't done so, but that defense attorney had a lot of specialized information that seemed suspicious to Arias.

Ever since then, she had been too cautious, at least in the Old Man's words. He had his personal notes on his tablet, but everything else for this case was on hers—not because she had taken over, but because the Old Man hated having her nag him.

The Old Man opened the door to his office, and tossed his tablet on the desk. He grabbed the suit jacket he'd worn two days before, and flung it over his arm.

Then he saw her glaring at him, and sighed.

"No one can understand my notes," he said. "They're in—."

Then he stopped himself and sighed again.

"Never mind." He grabbed the tablet, stuck it in a drawer, and punched the automated lock. "Satisfied?"

Not really. Those locks weren't solid. But this was a small victory, and right now, as tired as she was, she'd take it.

"Yeah," she said. "I'd offer to buy you a drink, but I think any alcohol would just put me to sleep."

He chuckled. "I stopped drinking during trials years ago."

She wasn't sure she knew that. She adjusted the strap for her own bag on her shoulder, and then followed him out of his office. She didn't even want to check hers.

They threaded their way through the maze of desks and old couches in the bullpen. Arias didn't see anyone sleeping on any of the couches, but she wasn't really looking. It wasn't that far to her apartment, but it felt like she had a journey as long as the one the *Renegat* had taken.

"There you are!"

The voice, strident and unmistakable, belonged to Anyi Etamè, one of the junior prosecutors helping with the case. She weaved her way to through the tables, waving a closed fist.

"You have to see this!"

"Who does?" Arias asked. She was so tired. She didn't want to see anything, and she hoped against hope that Etamè was talking to someone else.

"You both. Can we go to the office?" Without waiting for an answer Etamè walked around them and headed back to the Old Man's office. He hadn't locked the door.

Etamè flicked on a light as if the room was hers. She treated everything that way. Some of it was age: she had gotten her degree only a few years ago, but she was at least twice as old as most of the regular prosecutors. Law was her fifth career.

She wore flowing caftans that were always fresh and crisp, no matter what time of day Arias saw her.

Arias had picked Etamè as one of the people to watch the defendants, primarily because Etamè had an amazing talent. She could become motionless. People noticed her at first, particularly if she spoke, because of that forceful, nasal voice, but if she remained silent, they forgot she was around.

Both Arias and the Old Man followed her into the office. The Old Man seemed less perturbed by the invasion than Arias would be.

He entered last and pulled the door closed.

Etamè shoved some tablets and clothing and mugs away from the corner of the desk. The Old Man didn't seem to mind. Arias wanted to tell Etamè to stop that.

"You hit something," Etamè said. "That testimony today? It struck a nerve."

Suddenly, Arias was awake. Dauber's testimony had been the only testimony all day long.

"What part?" Arias asked.

"The interview," Etamè said. "Watch this."

She set the tiny tablet she had in her fist down on the edge of the desk, then tapped the top of the tablet. A holo of the overflow room appeared in miniature, making everyone look like tiny dolls sitting in tiny chairs.

Etamè used her fingers to enlarge, and then enlarge some more, until the image only showed a pint-sized Serpell watching the testimony.

Arias heard her voice, then Chief Judge Kanberra, and finally Dauber, setting up the interview.

Serpell didn't move through most of that, but when the interview started, she squirmed. Her face changed color as she watched herself lie to Captain Dauber well over a year ago.

Then Serpell put her head down, and she didn't move as everything wrapped up. Kabac, Gajra Blaquer, and Declan Connolly approached her after Chief Judge Kanberra gaveled down the day's session, and it was clear that the others looked furious.

Kabac in particular loomed over Serpell as if he wanted to strike her somehow.

Then something happened and he shook his head.

"What was that?" the Old Man asked.

Etamè reversed it. Serpell's voice, very faint, came through with a *Not now.* When the others didn't move, she repeated it, and they left.

She remained in the same position for a long time. Then she stood, her legs wobbling. She looked like someone who had just heard terrible news—like the death of a lover or the fact that they were going to prison.

Which she would be, if Arias had her way.

"Ha!" the Old Man said. "We got her! She's worried now."

So was Arias.

"Yeah, she is," Arias said. "And that 'not now' bothers me. Does it mean they've been meeting throughout this trial?"

Contrary to orders. Not that orders seemed to matter for this bunch.

"I haven't seen or heard anything," Etamè said, "but I haven't been watching them after hours. You want me to stick around?"

Arias looked at the Old Man. She wanted that to be his call, not hers.

"No," he said. "They have the right to meet without us."

"Even if they're discussing the strategies for their crime?" Etamè asked.

Arias spoke before the Old Man gave Etamè his famed *You haven't thought this through, have you?* lecture. Arias didn't need to hear that again.

"They don't control the trial," she said. "Even if they want to change the strategies, they have to work with Mukasey, and I doubt she'll change mid-trial."

"Yeah, that's what I thought," Etamè said, with a sideways glance at the Old Man. Apparently, she had thought it through then, and just wanted some confirmation. "All right. All I know is that Raina Serpell's reaction puts us on the right course."

Arias suppressed a surge of irritation. Of course they were on the right course. The key was convincing the judges of that.

The Old Man went to the door and held it open. Etamè left, and then he closed the door.

"We can change strategies right here," he said, "and go after the ringleaders. We have more than enough evidence to convict them when you combine the data and Dauber's testimony."

"Serpell maybe," Arias said.

"And others. Kabac, who did know the systems well enough to scrub them, but haphazardly, which seems to be how he did his job." The Old Man nodded, as if convincing himself. "And at least a dozen others."

"That's not enough," Arias said. "We leave the rest unprosecuted, and they'll make martyrs out of the ones who are. After all, those folks got them back here."

"Fat lot of good that did them," the Old Man said.

"That bothers you?" Arias asked. "The fact that they returned when they could have gone anywhere else?"

"No," he said. "They're not adventurers, not a one of them. This was a last-ditch effort to save their careers, not a trip they wanted to take. People like that, they don't think outside the box. Some of them aren't even aware of the box."

Arias smiled at him. He did not smile back. She let her smile fade.

"I don't want to change strategies," she said.

"Good," he said. "Because I want to be done with this case, and changing strategies would mean that we would have to reschedule everything."

He stretched, yawned, and then pulled the door open.

"Go home," he said to her. "Stay away from these couches. I want you fresh in the morning."

She barked out a laugh. "I won't be fresh for a long time," she said. "But I promise to sleep. I'll be as clearheaded as I can."

"Good," he said, "because we have a lot of trial to go."

TWENTY-ONE

The prosecution's case continued. Data, more data, people to establish how the data was used. People to discuss the psychology of the defendants. Other people talking about Fleet life one hundred years ago.

Mukasey was constantly taking notes, staying up late at night and revising her strategy. The one favor that the prosecution had done for her had been to show the judges just how extreme the situation was, just how hard it was for this entire group to survive the trip *to* the Scrapheap, let alone the trip back.

Mukasey would use that. She would use a lot of it.

But, after nearly a week of daylong testimony, she could see the judges getting tired. They had already made up their minds.

She would have to change their minds. And that would be a tall order. But she had retired Admiral Gão to help with that.

Mukasey decided to start with Gão, since the mission had started with her. That would change the narrative quite a bit.

The prosecution rested on the ninth day of the trial, and Mukasey began her case bright and early in the morning on the tenth day. She didn't sleep much the night before, changing and revising her plan.

She wasn't as good an orator as the Old Man. The real key for her case was to let the judges know that her perspective was different. If she droned on or if she threw too much data at them, she would lose them.

The judges would appreciate the brevity. Everyone involved in this trial would.

That morning, the courtroom was bathed in fake sunlight. The lighting changed daily, just like it did on the rest of the starbase. Too many people locked themselves in rooms and got no real light at all.

She wished the lights were dimmer, though, since she would probably be showing some holos by the end of the day. She supposed she could ask the court clerk to get the lighting changed, but she didn't want to call attention to it.

She just needed to focus and do her job.

She nearly lost her focus when she entered, and saw the fifty defendants already in their seats. Someone had brought them early and, worse, they had included Yusef Kabac. He sat in the front row like the creepy slug he was, arms crossed over his chest, his ill-fitting clothing looking even more inappropriate than usual.

He had had visible reactions to a lot of the testimony in the past ten days, even approaching Raina Serpell after Captain Dauber's testimony. It had seemed to Mukasey's assistant that Kabac wanted to discuss the testimony with Serpell, who had been visibly shaken by watching footage of herself talking to the captain on the *Aizsargs.*

Kabac and his terrible attitude was not what Mukasey needed this morning. The judges weren't in yet, but the prosecutors were. They had their heads together and were talking about something—or maybe talking about nothing, and just trying to unnerve her.

That conversation might have done so, if she didn't have Kabac to worry about.

She thought about how she would handle this, and then decided she wouldn't. She left the courtroom through a side door, searching for the clerk.

The clerk was a small man who struck her as unusually fussy. He made sure that everything was in its place before the day's events started, and he would occasionally hold up the judges if something was awry.

Mukasey had not spoken to him throughout this entire trial. The prosecutors had made some requests of him, but she hadn't.

That changed today.

He was standing before the door leading into the judges' wing, looking at a tablet of his own.

Mukasey didn't excuse herself or say his name to draw his attention. She just waited until he saw her.

"Yes?" he drawled.

"I was wondering if you could do me a favor," she said.

"I don't do favors," he said.

She bit back a response. She had simply used the sentence to be polite.

"I was wondering if it would be possible to have the first row of defendants move to the last row, and have the last row up front."

"Whyever would I do that?" the clerk asked, his eyes narrowed.

She had gone through the options in her head before she had talked to him, trying to come up with an excuse without mentioning Kabac. On her way to find the clerk, she had finally decided to appeal to his fussy nature.

"I thought I would be polite," she said. "I'm going to move them around anyway, with or without your help. But it's your courtroom, and I didn't want to step on any toes. If you don't want to make the switch, I'm happy to talk with them."

And then she turned her back on him. She hadn't even started to walk away when he said, "Wait. I'll do it."

Then he sighed heavily, stood, and disappeared through one of the side doors that led into the gigantic courtroom.

Now no one would know why the groups were switched around, which was good. She didn't need to antagonize Kabac any further. They already disliked each other. She didn't want to make that worse.

By the time she made it back into the courtroom, the shuffle was complete. Kabac sat in the far back corner, arms crossed over his increasingly massive stomach. His eyes glared over his bushy beard.

Mukasey turned her back on him and the rest of the defendants. Yes, she was arguing for their futures, but she couldn't think about that any longer. She needed to concentrate on her part of the case…and they weren't going to like much of what she was going to say.

She was standing when the door to the judges' chambers opened.

She sat down hurriedly, nearly losing her balance because the chair had turned away from her. Falling off her chair would have been a great way to start the day.

She touched her bracelet to center herself. She hadn't fallen, and all would be well.

The judges filed in. Every single one of the judges looked at her pointedly as they entered the courtroom.

She couldn't tell if the looks came from the fact they had discussed her or because she was on deck this morning or because they were warning her to wrap up the case quickly.

All of the judges adjusted their own tablets as they sat down, then folded their hands and looked over the courtroom expectantly. It seemed to her that they were keeping track of which defendants appeared when, something she hadn't planned on, and something that she didn't much like.

But she couldn't control everything—just her part of the case, and she was ready to start that.

Chief Judge Kanberra launched into his morning speech, mostly directed at the defendants, reminding them they did not have the right to speak in this court. Only Mukasey could speak for them.

Then he nodded at her, and she smiled back, hoping she didn't look as nervous as she felt.

She thanked him, and called her first witness—Judge Bella Gão. Normally, Mukasey didn't think of Bella Gão as an active judge, just as a retired admiral. But she wanted Gão's credentials up front, so that the other judges would give her testimony extra weight.

The back door to the courtroom opened, and Gão entered. She was a tiny woman whose perfect posture made her seem younger than she was. Her hair was clipped short and cupped her cheeks. Her gaze remained on the other judges and her expression was impassive.

She wore her admiral's uniform, with its silver and black retirement bars making her shoulders seem wider. Silver and black meant that she had served with distinction and retired with honors.

The uniform seemed a bit loose and it was nearly eighty years out of date, making it a great choice to illustrate some of the points she was going to have to make.

Gão sat in the witness chair, and looked around, as if she was trying to orient herself in the cockpit of a new ship. Clearly, she hadn't been in the witness chair in these courtrooms on Starbase Sigma. She had only seen the chairs from above.

Mukasey walked carefully over to the chair, so that she didn't upstage Gão. Gão had made an amazing entrance. Mukasey didn't want to spoil it.

When Mukasey reached Gão's side, she smiled. Gão nodded without a smile, making her seem even more formidable—or maybe just as judicial as the others on the bench.

"Please state your name and rank at retirement," Mukasey said. They hadn't had much practice. Gão had said she didn't like listening to practiced testimony as a judge, so she refused to do much.

She had twice told Mukasey to trust her.

Mukasey had had no real choice but to do so.

"Admiral Bella Gão, Retired," Gão said.

"You have moved to a new position, is that true?" Mukasey asked.

"I am now a judge in the Fleet system," Gão said.

"You turned down your most recent assignment. May I ask why?" Mukasey asked.

"Because I was assigned this case," Gão said. Murmurs echoed through the courtroom.

Mukasey had to use every bit of control she had to make sure she did not look at the defendants or the judges.

Gão made that somewhat easy by not taking a breath, even as the people in the courtroom reacted.

Instead, she continued, "I turned the case down because it would create an ethical burden for me. I am privy to information my colleagues are not. So I cited conflict of interest, which is how you found me."

"Yes it is," Mukasey said. "Why did you not contact me or the prosecution directly?"

"Because the *Renegat's* entire mission needed to be investigated," Gão said.

"And you think a legal case will be investigation enough?" Mukasey asked.

"It is perhaps the only remaining option," Gão said.

In some respects, she was the perfect witness. She did not elaborate. But Mukasey wanted her to elaborate.

"Why do you think the entire mission needed to be investigated?" Mukasey said.

"Because it was mishandled from the start," Gão said.

"How do you know this?" Mukasey asked.

"Because I was the person who was in charge of the *Renegat's* mission," Gão said.

More gasps, but none from the prosecution table. They seemed calm. They were expecting this. The gasps had come from the defendants.

The judges seemed to have themselves under control. For the first time in days, they looked interested.

"I was a vice-admiral at the time," Gão said, "and I was not allowed to turn down this assignment."

"You tried?" Mukasey asked.

"I not only tried," Gão said, "I also tried to have the mission scuttled."

"Why?" Mukasey asked.

"Because it was set up wrong," Gão said. "May I explain?"

"Please," Mukasey said. "Unless, of course, there are other objections."

The Old Man leaned back, his hands folded like the judges' hands. Arias watched, eyes hooded.

The defendants had moved a lot. They were sitting at attention. Mukasey almost looked at Kabac, but managed to stop herself in time.

"No objections," Chief Judge Kanberra said. "Proceed."

Gão nodded at him.

"At the time the *Renegat* was launched, I was the vice-admiral in charge of Scrapheaps," Gão said. "When I received notice from a Scrapheap that we had never heard of before, one that did not exist in our records, that it had been invaded and ships had been stolen, I went to my superiors to ask what they wanted done."

"This included Admiral Shannon Hallock, did it not?" Mukasey asked.

Gão glared at Mukasey. Apparently Gão did not like the interruption. "It did," Gāo said, a bit begrudgingly. "I shall get to her in a minute."

She turned her attention back to the judges. She was talking to them, and them only.

"In those days, normal procedure when notified of an unauthorized break-in at a Scrapheap was that we would send at least two DV-class vessels to investigate. Back then, we housed Ready Vessels in the Scrapheaps, behind layers of security so that no one could access those vessels without authorization."

Then she paused and looked at the panel. "I trust my colleagues know about Ready Vessels and Scrapheaps?"

Eight judges did. The rest did not.

So Gāo launched into an explanation of Ready Vessels, how, at the time, the Fleet had assumed they would travel backwards to fight wars against cultures that threatened them. The Ready Vessels were brand-new warships, staged for a fight.

Only in the entire existence of the Fleet, no Ready Vessel was ever used as intended.

"It is because of the *Renegat*," Gāo said, "that I was able to change the policy on Ready Vessels. We no longer house them in Scrapheaps."

The judges nodded, and Mukasey did not ask for an elaboration, even though she normally would have.

"I did not want to send *any* ships back to that Scrapheap," Gāo said. "The journey was dangerous and the incursion happened years before. If someone had planned to threaten us with Ready Vessels, they would have done so already."

"Why did no one listen to you?" Mukasey asked.

Gāo shot her an irritated look. "They listened to me. The problem was Admiral Hallock. She wanted to shut down all Scrapheaps and send ships back to destroy them."

Yet another collective gasp. This time, even the Old Man looked surprised.

"She wanted evidence from this mission to prove that Scrapheaps are untenable. She believed all out-of-date ships should be destroyed," Gāo said.

"I don't understand," Mukasey asked, just like she had the first time she discussed this with Gão. "How would this mission accomplish that?"

"She wanted to know how devastating the incursion was into that ancient Scrapheap. The fact that we had forgotten it added fuel to her fire," Gão said. Then she trained her gaze directly on Chief Judge Kanberra. "The other admirals did not want to risk DV-Class vessels, so we figured out what kind of ship would be needed to travel that distance."

This time, the chief judge moved. He leaned forward.

"It seems to me," he said, "that an SC-class vessel is ill-suited for this trip."

"It is," Gão said. "At the time, SC-class ships were designed to work in pairs. This ship had to go alone."

"Why is that?" Judge Bastien asked.

"Because no one thought it would return," Gão said.

"*What?*" Mukasey recognized that voice. It belonged to Kabac.

The Chief Judge banged his gavel. "Quiet," he said.

Someone grunted, almost angrily. Mukasey had a hunch she knew who that someone was.

Gão didn't seem to notice the interruption or the gaveling. Maybe being a judge had given her the ability to ignore other things in the courtroom.

And then she spoke without being prompted.

"I was to staff the ship with the idea in mind that the chances of return were very slim, maybe none," Gão said. Her brutal words resounded in the nearly silent courtroom.

Mukasey knew this was where the difficulties were going to come.

"I was told to use people who wouldn't be missed," Gão said. "They needed to be good at their jobs, I was told, but without family or even close friends. People who didn't fit in. I worried that they couldn't work together, if that was the case, but I was overruled."

More stirring.

"To be frank," Gão said. "I received a long list of possible crew members. Most refused the trip."

"We were ordered to go!" a woman shouted.

Chief Judge Kanberra banged his gavel again. "*Quiet!*"

"Yes," Gão said in response to the woman, "you were ordered to go, because we couldn't fill the ship otherwise."

Then Gão looked directly at the judges, her eyes glistening.

"I cannot tell you how much I regret this incident in my career." Her voice was soft. "I did try to abort the mission, when it became clear that all of those foldspace trips were creating a time lag."

She brought that up earlier than they had planned. Mukasey decided to let Gão take the lead.

"You did?" Mukasey asked.

"Yes," Gão said. "First, let me tell you about Captain Preemas."

Oh, good. She remembered the setup. Maybe she was better at catching the judges than Mukasey thought, because the judges were leaning in, interest on all of their faces.

"Ivan Preemas had more writeups than many of the other possible captains for the *Renegat*," Gão said. "However each writeup ended with the fact that he was a creative and talented captain. His attitude was terrible and he had trouble following orders, but he was a strong leader."

She took a breath, then settled back. Now, the courtroom was quiet.

"I met with him. He was rude and dismissive and angry. I did not like him, but he told me in no uncertain terms that he wanted the job. He pointed out that we needed a strong leader because the ship would be so very far from the Fleet. We needed someone who could handle the situation."

She made eye contact with all of the judges individually before continuing.

"After meeting with him, I went to Admiral Hallock again, and asked to cancel the mission. This was, to the best of my recollection, the third or fourth time I made that request. I was denied again."

"So the *Renegat* had to leave?" Mukasey asked.

"Yes," Gão said. "I was heartened by one thing: Nadim Crowe had chosen his own engineering team. They were good. They fit the criteria, as did Crowe, but they were a talented bunch, with a handful of exceptions."

Mukasey let that hang, because she didn't want to draw attention to Kabac right now. She would if she had to, to show that he didn't get along with Crowe, but she didn't want to establish that Kabac was trouble from the start.

Gão looked down at her hands. "For a while, Captain Preemas and Nadim Crowe worked together. That fell apart, though, over time."

"Do you know why?" Mukasey asked.

"The trip had become dangerous. The time lags that I mentioned are a sign that a ship is not just traveling through space, but that it's also traveling in time. I was worried that the ship might not reach the Scrapheap and still be in our time period."

Gão shook her head, clearly distressed.

"I finally spoke to Captain Preemas about this," she said. "Our foldspace communications at that point had a long enough lag to make the conversation frustrating—"

"Do you recall how long the lag was?" Judge Velsia asked. It took a moment for Mukasey to understand why Velsia was asking. She had served on ships that routinely traveled through foldspace. She understood the calculations.

"Not without looking it up," Gão said. "It was minutes, maybe ten, maybe fifteen, using a communication *anacapa* drive on the *Renegat* itself. I was afraid we would lose them and not be able to communicate."

"Isn't that what happened?" Judge Velsia asked.

"Not exactly," Gão said. "When the *Renegat* returned, the one thing I did learn was that someone had sabotaged the communications *anacapa*. But I get ahead of myself."

And she was ahead. There was so much to tell, and no real way to encapsulate it.

"Someone?" Judge Velsia asked. "You don't know who?"

"I do know who," Gão said. "It was Captain Preemas himself."

The judges leaned back in surprise. Arias dropped her head slightly, as if she hadn't known that. The Old Man continued to sit rigidly in place.

"In my last conversation with Captain Preemas," Gão said, "I ordered him to abandon the mission and to return to the Fleet immediately. He argued with me."

Gão looked at Mukasey. "Is it possible to show them this, rather than have me explain it?"

Gāo knew that Mukasey had recordings of all of Gāo's conversations with the *Renegat.* And Mukasey was ready for this one. She had asked that they set it up this way. It was better for the judges to hear directly from Preemas and to see what was going on.

"Yes," Mukasey said. "Let me get ready."

She hurried to her table, because they were getting close to the lunch break and she wanted to end with this.

She brought the tablet that had the holo recordings on them. She opened the file marked *Preemas.*

"Your Honors," she said as she sat that tablet on the arm of the witness chair. "This material has been altered. We have speeded up the time lag in between both sides of the conversation. You will see each side waiting, but you will not have to sit through about ten minutes of lag each time someone speaks. I can give you the unchanged files as well."

"Please do," Judge Velsia said before the chief judge could speak.

"All right," Mukasey said. "Here we go."

She started the holo recording.

A much younger Gāo stood in an alcove in the Engineering section of her ship, the *Správa.* Mukasey mentally kicked herself. She had forgotten to set up the reason that Gāo was in that tight alcove. It was because communications had already become nearly impossible.

Captain Preemas sat in the dark at a desk. He was hard to see, a ghost of a man, which Mukasey found creepy every single time she watched this, especially since she knew how he was going to die.

Light came up in his area. He was wearing his uniform, but his hair was getting unruly. His bright green eyes shone with intelligence and what Mukasey took to be fury.

Mukasey skipped a lot of the information holo-Gāo discussed with Preemas about the Scrapheap. Mukasey had a hunch that the judges would listen to the entire conversation anyway, and there was no need to add that into this very long day.

Instead, she began with the discussion of foldspace.

It was clear that holo-Gāo had been talking before this excerpt, but Mukasey didn't try to set up this part of the conversation. Instead, she let holo-Gāo talk.

"The time lags disturb me, Captain Preemas," holo-Gāo said. *"They're*

getting worse, not better, and we don't know what's causing them. There is a possibility that they're being caused by actual time displacement. You might have lost minutes as you traveled through foldspace. My concern is that the Renegat *will lose days next, then months, and then years. That will do us no good, Captain. We will have sent you back, you will have lost time, and we won't be able to communicate any longer. This entire mission is predicated on the fact that you have to find out what's going on at that Scrapheap and let us know what, if anything, that something is. It doesn't appear you can do that."*

It was also clear to everyone in the courtroom that holo-Gão had been right. Everything she said in that single discussion had come to pass. What Mukasey hadn't said was that the *Renegat* had only made four foldspace trips when Gão had this conversation with Preemas. The *Renegat* would make many more trips after this.

The other thing Mukasey didn't mention, because she didn't have to, was the fact that Preemas had been getting angrier and angrier as holo-holo-Gão talked.

"So, Captain Preemas," holo-Gão had, *"rather than continue on this mission, I am ordering you to bring the* Renegat *back to the Fleet. We will deal with the Scrapheap in some other way."*

"Oh my God," one of the female defendants said.

"What the—?" another said.

And someone started sobbing, quite loudly.

This time, Chief Judge Kanberra looked at all of them with compassion. Apparently, they hadn't known that they could have gone home, long before their nightmare had gotten worse.

"I need you to acknowledge that order," holo-Gão had said. *"I will be sending the official order at the end of this communique."*

Captain Preemas's skin had become mottled. He looked furious. For a moment, it seemed like he wouldn't answer her at all. This section always made Mukasey very tense, even though she knew what the man had done.

"Beg pardon, ma'am." He hadn't sounded like a man who was asking for forgiveness. He sounded as furious as he looked. *"But I'm the officer on the ground. I'm not seeing the problems that you are. My crew now works well together. I have gotten rid of most of the dead*

weight. They remain at Sector Base Z for someone else to waste time with."

"What?" someone asked. "The dead weight? Those people—"

"Shush," someone else whispered.

Their conversation could not drown out Preemas's voice. *"I moved others to different positions more suited to their skills. The ship now runs the way a ship should run."* He raised his chin. *"I think we are more than suited to this mission. I would ask you to rescind that order, ma'am. We deserve a chance to finish this mission."*

"Oooooh," one of the first voices said. They sounded relieved. Apparently that person believed that Gão had listened to Preemas.

"I appreciate your candor, Captain Preemas," holo-Gão was saying. *"I am glad you alleviated some of my concerns about your crew. However, you did not address the time lag. You will have to travel through foldspace four more times just to return to us. That's all the risk I'm willing to take. We are seeing an actual problem here, not a theoretical one, and therefore, I am aborting this mission."*

"What?" That was more than one voice. Several people were speaking at once, shouting, "No!" and "This can't be true!"

Finally Chief Judge Kanberra brought his gavel down hard.

"If you can't be quiet," he said, "I will toss you all from this room."

The voices faded, although several people were doubled over. Sobs echoed faintly in the chamber.

Apparently Kanberra wasn't going to worry about the criers.

Preemas had been shifting his weight. He had been so angry it was still palpable, all these years later.

"I don't understand your concern now, Vice Admiral," he said angrily. *"You were willing to send us to our deaths to garner some information for Admiral Hallock. And now you're telling me you're concerned about our lives? Forgive me if I don't believe you."*

Holo-Gão had not reacted to his insubordination. Her face had been remarkably impassive.

The current Gão was shaking her head slightly, apparently still unable to understand what that man had done.

Preemas's voice grew more strident. *"You're telling me that you don't believe you'll get the information from us, so we should return. It's the infor-*

mation you value, not our lives. Don't make this about us. Here's the truth, Vice Admiral. You didn't think the mission would fail before we got to the Scrapheap. As long as it looked like we'd get there and you could find out what the hell happened a century ago or whenever that breach occurred, you were fine with losing an entire ship full of misfits. But now that it's become clear that you might lose the ship without garnering a bit of information, you want us to return. Failure is failure only when the mission doesn't get accomplished, not when the crew dies. Am I right, Vice Admiral?"

Holo-Gão's only reaction had been a small one. She lifted her chin, giving her an air of complete authority and power.

"You have your orders, Captain Preemas," she had said. *"Abort this mission."*

The sobbing grew louder. The courtroom door banged. Mukasey looked at the defendants. At least three had fled, with more on the way, tears streaming down their faces.

She had known this would be a difficult day for them. She had been convinced of it. She had thought they would have trouble being described as failures and misfits.

She had not expected them to be so upset that Preemas had ignored the order to head back to the Fleet.

On the holo, Captain Preemas straightened. He tilted his head slightly.

"All right, Vice Admiral," he had said. *"Consider your mission aborted."*

And then his image winked out.

Holo-Gão stood perfectly still, as if she hadn't expected that reaction from him.

Mukasey shut off the holo, and turned to the current Gão.

"What happened next?" Mukasey asked.

"From my perspective," Gão said, "nothing. I didn't hear from them for a long time. Somewhere along the way, I realized that Captain Preemas had said he was going to abort the mission, but he wasn't going to come back to the Fleet."

"What do you think that meant?" Mukasey asked.

"I didn't know at the time," Gão said. "I still don't know."

"Do you think he was stealing the ship?" Mukasey asked. She tried not to sound too eager. That was one of her most important questions.

"Yes," Gāo said. "He had orders to return. He refused those orders. That made him a rogue operator. Had he been in the same sector, we would have brought security and more on him. He would have been arrested."

"But you couldn't do that because he was so far away," Mukasey said.

"That's correct," Gāo said.

"Couldn't you have sent some ships after him?" Mukasey said.

"No," Gāo said. "Remember, this mission was designed for loss. We were not going to put more ships and personnel into it."

Her words hung in the half-empty courtroom. Then Chief Judge Kanberra brought his gavel down, hard, making Mukasey jump. She hadn't expected it.

"This is as good a place to break for lunch as any," he said. "We have much to think about."

And then he stood. The other judges did too. They filed out one by one.

Mukasey let out a breath.

"I'll see you after lunch," she said to Gāo.

"Yes," Gāo said quietly. "You most certainly will."

TWENTY-TWO

"Well, that was a lovely defense," the Old Man said as he was striding toward his favorite restaurant in the justice wing. The restaurant didn't have a lot of privacy, which was one reason the Old Man liked it. It prevented long discussions over lunch.

This time, he seemed serious. He spoke of Mukasey's case with admiration, which wasn't quite where Arias had expected him to go.

She had to scurry to keep up with him. Other courts were letting out at the same time, and she envied those lawyers. They were dealing with mundane matters—a stabbing or a theft. She had the fate of 193 people and the future of the entire mutiny charge on her shoulders.

"Now we know how her case will play out," the Old Man said when Arias reached his side. "She will argue that they were trying to follow the Admiral's orders, and they were just trying to go home."

"It might work too," Arias said, a bit breathlessly. This sprint toward the restaurant always taxed her heart. "I'm not sure I can argue the other side."

"Even with the evidence in your favor?" the Old Man asked.

"We have to cross-examine Admiral Gāo carefully," Arias said.

"We're not cross-examining her," the Old Man said. "We're going to ask a few questions and then rebut her testimony. You'll reserve cross."

Arias looked at him. *That* was new. He was throwing surprises at her.

He saw her look, smiled, and winked. Then they reached the brown doors that led into the restaurant. He opened one, and swept his hand, indicating that she should go in first.

The minute she walked inside, this conversation ended.

She planted herself in front of the door. "You're going to explain this to me before the afternoon session, right?"

"No need," he said. "You'll see." And then he tilted his head toward the interior. "You going in?"

Of course she was going in. The tantalizing scents of garlic and ginger mixed with just a bit of soy made her stomach growl.

"If I'm blind," she said, "you're handing this."

"I know," he said, and followed her inside.

TWENTY-THREE

The line in the courtroom cafeteria was long, but Mukasey didn't have to go through it. The line existed only for people who did not work in the court—jurors, witnesses, observers. That included all fifty of that day's defendants from the *Renegat*.

Visitors with a pass got at least one free meal, and they usually used it at lunch.

The courtroom staff, like Mukasey, sat at a table, had their identification scanned, and the food they had ordered before they left their offices that morning just showed up.

Mukasey got a turkey sandwich with cranberry and cream cheese, a small piece of apple pie, and an entire carafe of coffee. Thank goodness the judges held a break every hour or two, because she would need it with all of the caffeine she was downing.

She was reviewing her notes for the afternoon when the food arrived. Someone or something had added chips of an indeterminate kind. Brown and curly and smelling faintly of onion. She set them aside and picked up the sandwich, trying to figure out whether she should let Gão talk about Nadim Crowe.

The morning had gone well. Mukasey didn't want to screw that up.

But someone would probably bring up Nadim Crowe, and Gão might just mention—

"What the hell do you think you're doing?" a man yelled from across the cafeteria.

She closed her eyes for a moment, wishing she had taken the turkey sandwich to go. She could have found a nice private room off one of the courtrooms to eat in peace. Because every single time she came to this cafeteria, someone lost their collective sanity about something. People were under a lot of stress here, and it showed in every single fiber of their being.

"Hey, you! Mukasey! Don't play dumb. You look at me!"

She started when the shouter mentioned her name. That was a first. She turned toward the voice.

Kabac was striding toward her, hands clenched in fists. His face was red, and his eyes looked like they were going to bug out of his head.

"You're ruining this case! What the hell are you thinking, making us sound like incompetent boobs. We got the *Renegat* home. We—"

"Shut up," she said as she stood. "If you want to talk to me as your attorney we will go into a meeting room. Otherwise, you are ruining privilege by talking to me here."

"Like it matters." His voice was lower now, but he was still talking much too loudly. "You just lost our case."

"You will come over here and talk to me like a human being," she said, "or I will call security and have you banned from this courtroom."

"You don't deserve to be talked to like a human being," Kabac said. He was shaking. He shoved up his sleeves as if he was going to use his hands for something.

Maybe something like beating her.

Her heartrate increased. She'd had clients threaten her but none of them actually looked like they could carry it out.

Kabac did.

Suddenly, court security was there. Two large people in the standard brown uniforms grabbed Kabac. She didn't even have to call them.

"Hey!" he shouted. "Heeeeey! You don't have the right to do this! Hey!"

He struggled, trying to break free.

"I understand he's your client," said a third person, a square-jawed woman with her hair cropped short. She wore a brown uniform as well. "Is he in custody somewhere?"

"Yes." Mukasey was proud of the fact that her voice was calm. "He's restricted to tower six. He's only here today as a defendant in a case. No one in our courtroom thought these defendants would be violent."

Although everyone involved in this case should have thought of that. Everyone. Because these 193 defendants were part of the battle for the *Renegat*, which killed and injured a lot of people.

"What do you want me to do with him?" the woman asked.

"Nothing!" Kabac yelled. "I have the right to talk to my attorney. I have the right to tell her what an idiot she's being. Talk about being an incompetent—."

One of the guards holding him shook him. "Shut the hell up."

Apparently they had done more than shake him—maybe tugged on his restraints—because he moaned and turned his head quickly from side to side, as if seeing the guards would make them less powerful.

"If he stays violent," Mukasey said, "you can treat him like any other violent defendant."

"Hey!" Kabac yelled as he tried to shake off the guards.

"Otherwise, take him to tower six. He has the right to watch these proceedings. Maybe work with the staff there to let him have his right to witness his accusers, but keep him away from the other defendants."

"All right then," the woman said. She turned and snapped her fingers at the guards. They jerked Kabac, trying to get him to move.

His gaze was on Mukasey though.

"You want me out of here because you screwed up the case so bad that you don't want anyone to point it out. You are worse than worthless. You—"

"I said shut up," one of the guards said, "or we will shut you up."

"You have no right," Kabac said to the guards.

"That's where you're wrong," the woman said. "There are different regulations governing the court wing. You have violated at least three of them, and if you don't settle down, we will shut you down."

Apparently that got through to Kabac, because he stopped yelling. But he continued to stare at Mukasey, as if he wanted to harm her.

The guards dragged him out.

The cafeteria was silent. Everyone was staring at Mukasey.

But she wasn't going to let herself shake. She wasn't going to let herself be upset about anything.

At least not visibly. And maybe not in reality.

She had a case to finish, not that Kabac had helped their cause. She had no idea how many court employees or bailiffs or security guards were in here, how many of the judges' clerks.

The judges never ate in this cafeteria, although many of them ordered up a meal from here, and often had a clerk bring it to them. Guaranteed someone would tell at least one of the judges about Kabac's outburst—how irrational he was, and how potentially violent.

Those kinds of things weren't supposed to influence a judge, but judges were human. No matter how hard the judge tried, that incident would factor into their decisions.

Mukasey sat down slowly. She had to finish her meal, not just for show, but because it would be a very long afternoon. She wouldn't be able to eat. She needed to be fortified.

She needed to be ready.

She needed to decide if she wanted to bring up Nadim Crowe. And if she did, she needed to figure out how to handle him.

Because his actions both helped and hurt her clients. If she could control the help part and minimize the hurt, she would win.

But that would take a lot of finesse on her part, and she wasn't even sure Admiral Gão would help with that.

TWENTY-FOUR

The courtroom was strange from the witness chair. Bella Gão was back in the chair, still astonished to be looking up at her colleagues on the bench. Sitting slightly below them did make them seem all-powerful. And the witness chair was raised a bit, so she sat higher than the lawyers did and certainly higher than the gallery.

Everyone had settled into their post-lunch discomfort. Some might doze if she wasn't interesting. Others might fiddle with the tech before them—at least the judges.

She had felt guilty about the *Renegat* for decades. She needed to get a few things off her chest before she finally passed away, and not just a random confession. She needed those things on a record—or, in this case, on what would probably become *the* record.

The defense attorney, Eun Ae Mukasey, stood rigidly beside the witness chair. Mukasey had argued before Gão before. Mukasey was a good enough attorney, maybe the best who would take a case like this. She wasn't great, but Gão was certain that the greats had probably turned this one down.

It smelled, and not just because Yusef Kabac had spent the morning shouting his dismay.

The more Gão heard about the case, the more she disliked the survivors. They seemed like a shifty bunch, but, she supposed, that was most likely her fault. She had chosen unlikeables, after all.

The afternoon part of the case started. Chief Judge Kanberra gave more instructions, mostly about remaining silent, no matter how shocking the testimony. That comment would have been directed at Kabac, but he was nowhere to be seen. Maybe Mukasey had ordered him back to his room or placed him in the off-site with the other survivors.

The remainder of the survivors looked a little different from the holos she had approved before the *Renegat* left, but not that different. The fact that Gāo recognized them all and could name them all individually after decades, showed her level of guilt.

She obsessed about that ship, and that was the one thing she would not discuss.

After Chief Judge Kanberra finished his second discourse of the day, Mukasey was finally free to continue her case. She turned to Gāo.

"I have one other topic to bring up with you," she said, "and this is only to put to rest some rumors."

Gāo nodded, even though she wasn't sure which rumors Mukasey referred to. Ever since the *Renegat* had returned, there were a thousand rumors about a thousand different things, many of them impossible to prove.

"I want to talk with you about Nadim Crowe," Mukasey said.

"All right." Gāo's breath caught, and she hoped that didn't turn up in her voice. Crowe still broke her heart.

"Before the conversation we saw with Captain Preemas," Mukasey said, "I understand you spoke to Nadim Crowe, who was then First Officer, is that correct?"

"Yes," Gāo said. "He contacted me about the problems the *Renegat* was having with the *anacapa* drives."

"Why didn't Captain Preemas contact you?" Mukasey asked.

No one objected, and someone should have. Mukasey had phrased the question wrong.

"I do not know," Gāo said primly. There was a risk for a sitting judge to answer questions. She had to follow the same rules that she usually enforced. "That would call for speculation."

"Did Nadim Crowe tell you why he contacted you?" Mukasey asked.

There it was. A question Gāo could answer.

"Yes," Gāo said. "The time lags concerned him, the problems with the communications *anacapa* drive concerned him, and he couldn't get through to Captain Preemas. He sent me data and asked that our experts here at the Fleet check the results. He believed that the time lags would get worse, and the *Renegat* could get lost in time. He asked that if the experts agreed with him, I would order the *Renegat* to return."

"Judging by your conversation with Captain Preemas, the experts agreed with Nadim Crowe," Mukasey said.

"Yes," Gāo said.

There was murmuring behind her. Even though she didn't like most of the survivors, she felt empathy toward them. It seemed this was the first time they had been told that their leaders had disagreed about whether to return to the Fleet in their time period. All that loss had to be hurting them, even if they had had no family to return to.

"Why did you trust Nadim Crowe?" Mukasey asked. "He had destroyed an entire Scrapheap when he was in school by being reckless."

"Yes, he did," Gāo said, "and he spent the rest of his career paying for it. He was a brilliant man, particularly on engineering issues. There was no one better to head to that ancient Scrapheap than Nadim Crowe."

"So why wasn't he sent back as captain?" Mukasey asked.

"Because his designation was Chief Engineer, which is where he should have stayed." Gāo straightened. The chair was suddenly uncomfortable. "The *Renegat* made an unscheduled stop at Sector Base Z and took on new crew members, letting some go. At that point, Captain Preemas changed many job designations, without my permission."

"You chastised him for that, did you not?" Mukasey asked.

"It was yet another point where I would have aborted the mission had I found out in a timely manner," Gāo said. "But Captain Preemas made sure I didn't get the information until he had gone through foldspace. He knew that we wouldn't use our resources to recover the *Renegat*."

"He sounds difficult," Mukasey said.

"He was insubordinate repeatedly," Gāo said. "I should have trusted my instincts and told Admiral Hallock that there was no one qualified to captain the *Renegat*."

"What would she have done if you had said that?" Mukasey asked. Then she caught herself before Gão could remind her that that question was speculation too. "Or rather, what were you worried that she would do?"

"I worried that she would either put someone else in charge of this mission or that she would bring in a captain who did not fit the criteria," Gão said.

"Meaning a captain with a family or highly credentialed, someone the Fleet didn't dare lose on a frivolous mission," Mukasey said.

Gão did not like that characterization. "Those are your words."

"What are yours?"

"I looked at every captain who fit the criteria," Gão said. "Ivan Preemas was the only one who had even a remote chance of getting that crew to the Scrapheap and bringing them back alive."

"He got them to the Scrapheap, did he not?" Mukasey asked.

"I don't know that for certain," Gão said. "Someone did."

She wasn't going to speculate in court, no matter how many times she had speculated in the silence of her apartment.

Mukasey finally seemed to realize that.

"Captain Preemas made Nadim Crowe first officer," Mukasey said. "That sounds like he trusted Crowe."

"I don't know," Gão said.

"But you trusted Crowe," Mukasey said.

"Yes."

"And when Nadim Crowe told you that the ship was having trouble, you confirmed the data he sent, and then ordered Captain Preemas to abort the mission, an order he disobeyed."

"Yes."

"And then what happened?" Mukasey asked, being maddeningly vague.

"On the *Renegat?*" Gão asked. "I don't know."

"In your office?" Mukasey asked.

"I had a hunch that Captain Preemas was not going to follow my instruction, based on his past behavior. I needed to talk with him again about the time lag. He did not answer my hails." Gão worked hard at keeping her voice neutral.

"He didn't answer or the messages didn't get through?" Mukasey asked.

"I don't know," Gão said. "At the time, I thought he was being insubordinate. Nadim Crowe had told me that I had to get back to him quickly before they went into foldspace again, so I had my staff attempt to contact Crowe by backtracing the channel he had used, and going through that."

"Did you reach him?" Mukasey asked.

Some of Gão's colleagues were leaning forward, clearly interested. So much for the post-lunch doze.

"No," Gão said. "We were never able to hail the *Renegat* again."

"My god," someone said audibly.

Kanberra looked at the defendants. "One more outburst and I will send you all out of the courtroom. Is that clear?"

Apparently, they nodded or gave some form of assent, because he waved a hand at Mukasey.

"Proceed," he said.

"But you heard from Nadim Crowe again, didn't you?" Mukasey asked.

"Yes." Gão heard the sadness in her own voice.

"When was that?" Mukasey asked.

"A message he sent in that time period reached me five years after the *Renegat* disappeared," Gão said.

"Can you explain how that happened?" Mukasey asked.

"Technically no," Gão said. "That is not my area of expertise. But it is not unusual for ships that have foldspace lag to have time lag as well. You'd need an expert to testify why five years and not shorter or longer. The salient point this: by the time the message reached me, it was much too late for me to do anything."

"At that point did you know about the battle for the *Renegat?*"

"No," Gão said. "All I knew was that the *Renegat* had been missing for five years."

"Do you know when Crowe sent the message?" Mukasey asked.

"According to the way he was experiencing time, he sent the message one month after my final conversation with Captain Preemas," Gão said.

"What did Nadim Crowe need to tell you?" Mukasey asked.

Gāo did her best not to glare at Mukasey. They had discussed this. Gāo did not want to parrot Crowe's words. She wanted Crowe to speak for himself.

"It would be better if I showed you what he said," Gāo said. She didn't want to watch it again—she never wanted to watch it again—but she had to. Because someone might ask her about it.

Mukasey turned to the judges. "We would like to show you the recording. I would like to enter it into evidence."

"So ordered," Chief Judge Kanberra said.

Gāo took a deep breath. She had a different tablet with Nadim Crowe's message cued up.

She started the holo, and resisted the urge to close her eyes.

She needed to watch this, one last time.

TWENTY-FIVE

A hologram of Nadim Crowe stood in the center of the courtroom. He was a tall rangy man with a foreboding face. Behind him, equipment glinted and glistened. He clearly wasn't on the bridge of the *Renegat* or in the captain's ready room.

Arias had seen a tiny version of this recording, but seeing it live in the courtroom was much more powerful. It was as if Crowe had shown up from the dead to give testimony.

From her place at the prosecutor's table, she could see some of the judges through the image, faint and attentive. It was almost as if she saw ghosts bleeding through the image of a ghost.

"Vice Admiral." Crowe's voice was raspy and deep. He looked exhausted. *"The situation on the* Renegat *has become dire. I waited to hear from you after our last contact, and heard nothing. I consulted with Captain Preemas, who told me that you had convinced him to forge on to the Scrapheap."*

A couple of the judges leaned back. To Arias's surprise, the defendants behind her were silent. No one was sobbing like they had that morning.

Crowe was saying, "*Later, I discovered that he had completely disabled our foldspace communications channel. If you have been trying to reach us, and cannot, that is why. In the meantime, he continued to tell me about the various conversations that you have had with him, conversations that I know could not and did not happen....*"

Now there was a faint response. Just one little "oh," from behind Arias.

Crowe held up his arm. He was black and blue.

"I am no longer in the command structure, although officially I am. I found out when, against my advice, Captain Preemas sent this ship into foldspace. He did so without warning any of us."

This time, Arias did look at the defendants behind her. A few were nodding. A couple were rubbing knees or ribcages. Phantom pain, probably, from injuries sustained at that time.

"The foldspace journeys have become more and more violent. I'm afraid the ship will shake apart in one of them. A number of us were injured this time."

Crowe went on to describe many of the injuries, as well as the other ways that Preemas had become more reckless instead of less.

"Vice Admiral Gão, I humbly request that you relieve Captain Preemas of duty. I ask that you do so by patching into our entire communications system shipwide. I would prefer not to do that myself, so that I won't be less compromised than I already am."

One of the judges glanced at the Old Man, to see his reaction. The Old Man and Arias knew about this, of course, and they were prepared. All that mattered now was how the judges reacted to this whole thing.

Still, this was hard to watch.

Crowe said, *"If you do not want me to run the ship, that is fine. You have a few other candidates who might be able to do a good job. I will assist whoever you choose."*

He shifted. He would have been a good witness had he come back with the crew. Of course, if he had come back, things might have been different.

And really, he was a witness. Maybe the best one in the entire trial.

Arias tried not to look away as he said the part she worried about the most.

"I am contacting you because I believe in the Fleet, in her rules and regulations, and in the proper way of doing things," he said.

That wasn't just the right thing to say. It was also completely sincere, and Arias couldn't cross-examine him.

Nor could she argue with his next points, about the fact that Captain Preemas was sabotaging the mission and that the ship might not survive. That so many people, from Gão to Crowe to others on the crew, knew that the *Renegat* was suffering time lag, meant that there was a serious survival issue at hand, an issue some might have assumed would be justification for the battle of the *Renegat.*

"I suspect you tried to send me the rest of the information that I requested, and that it did not arrive because of the captain's perfidy."

Arias suppressed a sigh. *Perfidy* was a heck of a word, probably deliberately chosen. It was clear, just from this single recording, that Nadim Crowe was a deliberate man.

"I am assuming that you also believe the communications anacapa *might be causing some of our lag. I have no idea if the lag remains, because of what Captain Preemas did. We are also two trips through foldspace past our last contact, so our data gathering isn't as clear as I would like it. That's why I am sending you this message on all channels that I possibly can, in as many ways as I can. It's not worth even trying to talk at the moment."*

His voice shook a little. He sounded like a cautious man driven to the end of his rope. He also sounded like a man who didn't want to admit he was terrified.

"Vice Admiral," he said, *"I hope you see fit to follow my advice. Please do let me know if I am overstepping."*

Of course he was overstepping. He was asking that the crew somehow demote a sitting captain. He was asking for Gão to help with that, but that might not have been enough.

"I hope you consider my proposal," he said. *"I hope to hear from you soon. Thank you for your time."*

And then his image winked out, his voice—deep and a bit strained—echoing in the courtroom.

"Is that the end of the recording?" Judge Ioannide asked. She sounded suspicious.

"Yes." Gão was the one who answered.

"Did you get any more messages from this Crowe?" Judge Ioannide asked. Arias couldn't read her, except to see that the judge was upset.

"No," Gão said.

"Was this before or after the mutiny?" Chief Judge Kanberra asked.

"I'll answer that," Mukasey said. "We put together a timeline. This was before."

She had saved Gão from answering a question that she had no knowledge of.

Chief Judge Kanberra nodded. No one else spoke, so Mukasey turned to Gão.

"What happened to Nadim Crowe?" she asked.

"Officially, I have no idea," Gão said.

"Unofficially?" Mukasey asked.

"I am not the person to ask," Gão said.

Nadim Crowe had not returned with the *Renegat*, one way or another. Everyone in the room knew that.

Mukasey turned toward the judges.

"That's all I have for this witness," she said, and returned to her seat.

"Mr. Yglesias?" the Chief Judge asked. "Do you or Ms. Arias have any questions for this witness?"

"Many, Your Honor," the Old Man said, without standing up. "But we would like to reserve them. We would like to call a rebuttal witness first."

Gão started. She seemed surprised that she could be rebutted.

"That's unusual," the Chief Judge said.

"This is an unusual case," the Old Man said.

The Chief Judge seemed to consider for a moment, and then he nodded.

"All right," he said. "We need a chair for Judge Gão. She needs to listen to rebuttal testimony if there are going to be questions for her afterwards."

Then he leaned forward a bit and smiled at Gão.

"You're dismissed for the moment," he said.

She smiled back at him, and for the first time, her lovely skin wrinkled. "Thank you, Your Honor."

She gathered her things, stood a bit unsteadily, and let one of the clerks help her to a chair someone had found.

She sat down, then frowned at Mukasey, as if asking what was coming next.

Mukasey gave an almost imperceptible shrug.

No one on that side knew what was next. Because the Old Man and Arias had buried the information in their discovery packet.

They had listed every single one of the 193 defendants as possible witnesses.

But they felt they only needed one.

Jorja Lakinas.

So Arias called her to the stand.

TWENTY-SIX

Mukasey was on her feet before she even realized she had stood up.

"I object! They have to go through me to get approval for one of my clients to testify, and no one spoke to me about it at all."

The judges all looked distressed as well.

"Mr. Yglesias," Chief Judge Kanberra snapped, "what are you thinking?"

"Ms. Lakinas is represented by Oscar Vaas, Your Honor, at least to my knowledge," the Old Man said calmly.

Mukasey clenched her fists. "No one informed me about the change in counsel." And she had expressly told her clients not to do that, because it would screw up her case, and it was. It was.

She made herself breathe. She was trying not to be furious, even though she was furious.

"Is Mr. Vaas here?" Chief Judge Kanberra peered into the gallery as if it was darker than the rest of the courtroom.

A man stood up just behind the prosecutor's table. Mukasey recognized him but hadn't known his name until now. She'd seen him around the courts because he had been hard to miss. With his green eyes, tight curls and general air of intelligence, he had always been hard to ignore.

"I'm Oscar Vaas, Your Honors," Vaas said, speaking very precisely. "I represent Jorja Lakinas on financial and health matters."

"I want you to remind you right now, Mr. Vaas, that you're speaking to the court as an officer of the court. If you lie or misrepresent in any way, you will be up on charges and possibly disbarred. Do you understand?"

"Fully, Your Honor," Vaas said calmly, as if he had expected that.

Mukasey was mentally kicking herself. She should have fought harder to placate that woman.

"Health and financial matters, eh?" Chief Judge Kanberra said, as if he was musing over something. "Are you aware of this, Ms. Mukasey?"

"Of her representation, no," Mukasey said. "I do not want one of my clients testifying."

"Then you're fired!" A voice yelled from the back.

Mukasey turned, as did the rest of the court. Jorja Lakinas sat near her cart, her body hunched. It seemed like she looked even more damaged than she had when Mukasey first met her.

Of course she did. Lakinas wanted something.

"Are you Jorja Lakinas?" Chief Judge Kanberra asked.

"Yes," Lakinas said, "and I'm firing her."

Lakinas used her good hand to point at Mukasey.

"You should have done so before this case got underway, Ms. Lakinas," Chief Judge Kanberra said.

"I'm sorry, Your Honor," she said, not sounding sorry at all. "I thought when I hired a new attorney, the old one would be notified."

"Only when they're working on the same case," Chief Judge Kanberra said. "Perhaps this is on you, Mr. Vaas. You should have informed her of the conflict."

"I told her I would not work on her defense here," Vaas said.

Mukasey was very confused. Her cheeks burned. She didn't need to be sandbagged like this.

"Then what are you doing here?" she asked.

"My thoughts exactly, counselor," Chief Judge Kanberra said. "But do allow me to express them."

There was amusement in his tone, which irritated her. Nothing about this was amusing. Nothing at all.

"I'm sorry, Your Honor," she said.

"My client wants treatment for her injuries, the treatment she is owed as a member of the Fleet," Vaas said. "So I went to the office of the prosecutor and talked with them. They wanted information in exchange. She decided to give them information which is, apparently, pertinent here."

"That's sideways and sneaky," Chief Judge Kanberra said. "You should have notified the court, Mr. Yglesias, Ms. Arias."

Yglesias spread his hands. "We did, Your Honor. She is on the witness list."

"No, she's not." Mukasey had been over and over and over the list. If she had seen Lakinas's name, she would have prepared.

"I don't see her on this list," Judge Ioannide said, somewhat accusingly.

"She's not listed by name," the Old Man said. "She's on the list as one of the one hundred and ninety-three."

Mukasey started to slam her fist on her desk and barely stopped herself. Son of a bitch, she had been sandbagged. Badly.

"All right then," Chief Judge Kanberra said. "Under these somewhat odd circumstances, I will allow the testimony without delay. Since she was one of your clients, Ms. Mukasey, you will not need time to prepare. You should know what she knows."

"That's a hell of an assumption, Your Honor," Mukasey said, then mentally kicked herself. She shouldn't have been that rude.

"I realize you just got caught in one of Mr. Yglesias's traps, Ms. Mukasey, but that does not entitle you to disrespect this court," Chief Judge Kanberra said firmly.

"Yes, Your Honor," Mukasey said. She'd learned long ago not to apologize for a terrible wrong, because if she did so, that might call more attention to it.

The Chief Judge wasn't even thinking of her any longer. He had just directed his clerk to call Lakinas to the stand.

Mukasey remained standing. Jorja Lakinas was exaggerating her symptoms. She moved slowly, her body hunched, and she looked like she was in pain.

And, to be fair, she was in very bad shape. But not this bad.

Mukasey made herself sit slowly before anyone noticed that she had been standing when she shouldn't have been.

She couldn't mention that Lakinas was exaggerating her injuries. She didn't dare mention that at all.

This entire testimony was filled with landmines. And contrary to what Chief Judge Kanberra had assumed, Mukasey had no idea what information Lakinas had.

Arias was handling this testimony. She carefully led Lakinas through the preliminaries, her full name, her rather ugly career, the fact that she had been on the *Renegat* from the beginning which meant she had been chosen by Admiral Gão.

Mukasey was making notes, mostly because she had no idea where this was going.

"How did you get so badly injured?" Arias asked Lakinas.

"I fought beside Captain Preemas and nearly died," Lakinas said.

"You were fighting *with* Captain Preemas," Arias said. "Against the mutineers?"

"Objection," Mukasey said with more force than necessary.

Arias held up a hand. "My mistake. Against…who, exactly?"

"The force Nadim Crowe put together," Lakinas said. "He wanted the ship. He *took* it really."

"How did he do that?" Arias asked. There had already been some testimony on this. Apparently the prosecution didn't think there had been enough.

"He barricaded himself and his friends in engineering, then shut off all of the access to the ship's controls. Only he could operate them." Lakinas still sounded mad about that.

"What did you do at that point?" Arias asked.

"Captain Preemas asked me and a few others to help him get weapons. We did. Then we went down to engineering. We were going to break in."

"With force?" Arias asked.

"No." Lakinas's voice was tight. "I was supposed to access the door commands from the corridor, but Crowe had even shut that down."

"Then what did you do?"

"I—We—tried to break down the door by using the back end of our weapons as battering rams."

"Did that work?" Arias asked.

"No," Lakinas said. Mukasey was right; Lakinas was still furious. She was glaring at the others in the courtroom.

"So what happened next?" Arias asked.

"Someone—India Romano, I think—"

"Raina Serpell's wife?" Arias asked.

"Yes," Lakinas said.

"She fought for Captain Preemas?" Arias asked.

"Yes," Lakinas said.

"And later died under mysterious conditions on the trip home?" Arias asked.

"Objection!" Mukasey shouted. "Where is this coming from?"

"Withdrawn," Arias said. She hadn't looked away from Lakinas, which angered Mukasey even more. "What did India Romano do?"

"She shouted 'fire!' or 'shoot it down' or something like that and we did and…" Lakinas stopped. For the first time, her strident voice hitched.

Mukasey held her breath. She knew this part.

"…and…" Lakinas took a deep breath. "…we were stupid. It was a killing box. The shots ricocheted off the doors, the walls. Crowe didn't have to fire a shot."

"And that's where you were injured?" Arias asked.

"I nearly died," Lakinas said.

"That's why you're here, right? To get treatment for those injuries?"

"Yes," Lakinas said. "I didn't get real treatment *ever*. No one on the *Renegat* helped me because I fought with Captain Preemas. They stopped the bleeding and kept me from dying and put me in the brig."

"And when you were rescued from the *Renegat*?" Arias said.

"I was put in with the rest of the—what do they call us? Renegades? And no one would give me medical help then either. They told me that we would learn what I was entitled to after the trial."

"Which trial?" Arias asked.

"This one," Lakinas spit out the words. "They wanted to know if I got Fleet medical care as a member of the Fleet or if I got minimal care as a criminal."

Then she glared at the judges.

"I am *not* a criminal. I fought for my captain," Lakinas said.

"Did you believe in his cause?" Arias asked.

Lakinas sat back, as if she hadn't expected that question. Then she said, "It doesn't matter what I believed. He was my captain. Someone was trying to take over his ship. He needed help stopping it."

"Let's be clear," Arias said. "You've been offered medical care in exchange for this testimony, is that correct?"

"Yes," Lakinas said. "Whether or not I get lumped in with the rest of these people and even if they're found guilty, I'm still getting the treatment I deserve as a member of the Fleet. *That's* why I decided to talk today. Because I can't be in this kind of pain any longer."

Mukasey swore under her breath. This was her fault. She should have taken care of Lakinas. Maybe a few others as well. And she probably should have pulled the troublemakers like Kabac out of the way.

"The information you have is about Nadim Crowe, isn't it?" Arias asked.

Mukasey started. This couldn't be good.

"Yes," Lakinas said. "And I brought my journals as backup. I kept a video journal when it became clear that no one was going to take care of me. They got pulled off the ship with all of the other data when we were rescued."

"*Objection!*" Mukasey said with as much force as she could. "I have not received any notice of these journals."

The Old Man gave her a sideways look and said, before the Chief Judge could say anything, "It's in all the documentation from the ship, Your Honors. She's had these journals just like the rest of us. It's not our duty to tell her where to look in the evidence."

There was so much evidence. More than a year of data, and she didn't know how to search it all. She also knew that the prosecution hadn't looked at all of it either.

The difference was that Lakinas had pointed them to the data and not to her.

"Overruled," Chief Judge Kanberra said. He gave Mukasey a warning look, as if she had performed badly for her clients.

She hadn't. She had done everything she could within reason.

But she felt sick. She still had no idea what had happened to Crowe aside from the vague comments her stupid clients had told her, but clearly that wasn't enough. Something bad had happened to him; she had known that all along, but she hadn't known what.

Clearly, the prosecution did.

"What happened to Nadim Crowe?" Arias asked.

"We left him behind," Lakinas said.

"What does that mean?" Arias asked.

"I mean deliberately. He and his engineers and the people he thought were competent were looking for a ship that was in good enough shape to handle all of us—"

"Where?" Arias asked.

"In that damn Scrapheap," Lakinas said. "We found it, and it was a disaster, but we were there. We had some repairs to do on the *Renegat*, and they were done enough, I guess. Because when Nadim Crowe took his favorites to that ship in the Scrapheap, the ship they were going to fix, we left them behind."

Someone moaned. Maybe it was even Mukasey. She had always suspected something like this.

"You left them behind? How?" Arias asked.

"The *Renegat* went into foldspace, and left them," Lakinas said.

"Deliberately?" Arias asked.

"Yes," Lakinas asked.

"Without food or water?" Arias asked.

"They had some. I heard that discussed. They had like a month's worth. People were laughing about it, saying that Crowe was so talented he could conjure up a working ship and get somewhere with food before his ran out."

The entire courtroom was silent.

"What do you think happened to them?" Arias asked.

Mukasey made herself object. "Speculation," she added.

"I'll allow it," Chief Judge Kanberra said, just like she expected him to.

"Oh, they died," Lakinas said. "What else could have happened?"

Arias let the assumption hang. Mukasey clenched her fists. There was no proof of murder, and yet the chief judge had just allowed everyone to assume it.

Arias stopped beside Lakinas. "You're convinced this was deliberate. What made you think that? Did someone tell you? Were you part of the decision?"

"*Me*?" Lakinas laughed. "I was still in custody at that point, although in my quarters because I was so ill."

"Then how do you know they left Crowe and his team behind on purpose?" Arias asked.

"Because they confessed on video," Lakinas said. "They wanted Crowe to know what they did. I have the recording."

Mukasey felt her heart sink. Her clients must have thought this was gone, with the ship.

Chief Judge Kanberra looked at her, as if he expected her to object.

She sighed. "Objection, Your Honor."

He nodded.

They both knew exactly how this was going to go. The information had been buried in the data somewhere.

"We disclosed this," Arias said. "It is not our fault that Ms. Mukasey does not take a thorough approach to the evidence."

"That was a cheap shot, Your Honors," Mukasey said. "They know I have a small firm, and they know that I'm being paid a small fee per client. It is not enough to—"

"We understand, Ms. Mukasey." Chief Judge Kanberra gave her a small sympathetic smile. "We also know that Mr. Yglesias's office is famous for following the letter but not the spirit of the rules."

"Your Honor!" Arias said.

He looked at Arias. "You have an objection, Ms. Arias?"

She clearly caught herself before going further. "No, Your Honor."

Mukasey felt a small mean joy inside her. At least *she* had Chief Judge Kanberra's sympathy, not Arias.

Fat lot of good it would do, though. This testimony was devastating.

"I'm sorry to tell you, Ms. Mukasey," Chief Judge Kanberra said, "but the objection is overruled."

She was not surprised. No one was. She really had no reason to object, nothing to really fight with.

"In that case," Arias said, "let's see this recording."

Lakinas put one of the small tablets on the arm of the witness chair. "This is the message they sent to Nadim Crowe as they went into foldspace."

"They," Arias said.

Lakinas nodded. "I sure as hell wasn't consulted."

She made it sound like she would have advised against it. She poked her forefinger hard onto the tablet, and a hologram snaked its way into existence.

A thinner Yusef Kabac appeared in the center of the courtroom. His eyes glistened manically. He was smiling. Mukasey had never seen him smile with such joy.

"We're heading back," holo-Kabac said. *"We don't want to stay here, and you're going to make us. No one on this ship now will be court-martialed. We'll be fine."*

Mukasey sank lower in her chair. She hadn't thought this could get worse, but it just did. Not only did Kabac cite the reason for leaving, but he also indicated that the entire crew had discussed court-martials for the overthrow of Captain Preemas.

Then Mukasey sat up. That might be the key. She might still have a case after all.

"Did anyone ask to return to the Scrapheap to rescue Crowe and the others left behind?" Arias asked.

"Not to my knowledge," Lakinas said. "But someone could have. I wasn't around the crew much."

"Did you ask?" Arias asked.

"I wasn't involved in the decision making. They thought I was the criminal."

"But they set you free, right?" Arias asked.

"Eventually," Lakinas said. "Not that it mattered. I had to stay in my quarters because I was so sick. I really wasn't any kind of threat to anyone."

Arias nodded once. "Thank you," she said. Then she turned to Mukasey. "Your witness."

Mukasey set her emotions aside. She had to. Otherwise her fury and frustration would destroy what was left of this case.

She made herself stand, and walked over to the witness chair. Lakinas looked at her with shining eyes, almost as if she was pleased she had gotten the better of Mukasey.

Mukasey decided not to care what Lakinas was thinking. "What did Yusef Kabac mean about court-martialing someone?"

Lakinas paused for a moment before responding, as if she thought maybe this was a trick question. Then she said, "There were people who weren't involved in what you're all calling the battle for the *Renegat*. They were doing their jobs somewhere else."

"Who are those people?" Mukasey asked.

"I'm not naming them all," Lakinas said. "But you have a lot of them as clients."

"So when the conversation turned to court-martial," Mukasey asked, "did everyone believe that the entire crew would be court-martialed?"

"I have no idea what everyone believed," Lakinas said.

"What did you overhear?" Mukasey asked, knowing she was treading on thin ground. The answers could go against her just as easily as they could go in her favor.

"A lot of the crew was angry that we were in this mess. A lot of them blamed Nadim Crowe for getting violent."

"Did you?" Mukasey asked.

"He tried to take over the ship," Lakinas said. "What do you think?"

"What I think doesn't matter," Mukasey said. "What you think does. Did you blame Nadim Crowe for the violence?"

"I think there were better ways to handle the conflict he had with Captain Preemas," Lakinas said.

"Did you hear Admiral Gāo's testimony?" Mukasey asked.

"What part?" Lakinas asked.

"There were two parts in particular," Mukasey said. "The part where Captain Preemas ignored Admiral Gāo's order to return to the Fleet—"

"Yeah, I heard that. She doesn't understand. Most of us knew it was our last chance to prove ourselves. We weren't going to go home." Lakinas's injured hand was shaking. Her voice was too.

"So he consulted with all of you about whether or not to turn around?" Mukasey asked.

"Not with me," she said. "I have no idea who he talked to. But I don't care. He was right to continue the mission. We'd already gone through a lot at that point."

Mukasey was not going to ask what "gone through a lot" meant. She didn't want to lose this thread by going off on a tangent.

"All right," she said. "Did you also hear the testimony from the admiral about her plans for Nadim Crowe? Did you see his holo where he asked her to step in and make him captain?"

"Yeah," Lakinas said. "So?"

"So it sounds like he and Captain Preemas could no longer agree on anything," Mukasey said.

"Then Crowe should've stood down. It wasn't his ship," Lakinas said.

"Did others on the crew feel that way?" Mukasey asked.

"I didn't do a poll," Lakinas said.

"In your experience," Mukasey said.

"My experience was pretty limited." She ran a hand over her body, as if to remind everyone just how injured she was.

Mukasey was losing the thread, whether she wanted to or not.

"What I'm trying to get to here," she said, "is why Yusef Kabac believed the court-martial issue was resolved when Crowe and all the others were left behind at the Scrapheap."

"Oh, that," Lakinas said. Apparently, she hadn't understood where Mukasey had been going with the questions. "That's easy. Everyone who actively fought on the side of Nadim Crowe was on that ship that got left behind."

A couple of the judges smiled ever so faintly. Apparently, they liked what they had just heard.

"So really, those who got left behind could have been considered mutineers, right?" Mukasey asked. "They were criminals, and since there was no way to deal with them, they got abandoned instead."

"Objection," the Old Man said. "If she wasn't testifying, I would say she's leading the witness."

"Except that she's your witness," Chief Judge Kanberra said.

"And her former client," the Old Man said.

"I'll rephrase," Mukasey said. "Did you consider them mutineers?"

"I considered every single fucking one of them my goddamn enemy," Lakinas said with such force that Mukasey almost stepped backwards. "They guaranteed that I'd be like this for the rest of my life. Nothing the Fleet can or will do will make me whole again. It's too damn late."

Mukasey couldn't improve on that.

"Nothing further," she said, and returned to her seat.

As soon as she sat down, Arias popped up.

"Redirect, Your Honor," she said.

"Make it short," Chief Judge Kanberra said. "It's been a long day."

Arias smiled at him, even though she probably wanted to strangle him. Mukasey would have in that circumstance.

Arias walked to Lakinas. "When Captain Preemas died, who ended up running the ship?"

Lakinas raised her head ever so slightly. "Nadim Crowe."

"Doesn't that make sense?" Arias asked. "The captain was killed. The first officer took over."

"The first officer caused the captain's death," Lakinas said.

"Not according to your testimony," Arias said. "The fact that you all shot your weapons in what you called a killing box caused the captain's death."

Lakinas didn't respond to that.

"By Fleet regulations," Arias said, "the first officer becomes captain when the real captain dies. Did Captain Preemas demote Nadim Crowe before the battle?"

Lakinas looked sullen. "Not to my knowledge."

"It's not in the records either," Arias said. "Which means that Crowe was the acting captain of the *Renegat*, and he knew it, right? He acted on it. He was running the ship, correct?"

"Yes," Lakinas said tightly.

"And you know this for a fact, right?" Arias asked.

"Yes," Lakinas said, even more tightly.

"*How* do you know this as a fact?" Arias asked.

"Because," Lakinas said looking down, "he told me that, as acting captain, he wasn't going to let me out of the brig. He said I could get the medical attention I needed where I was."

Her lip curled downward.

"That was a lie," she said.

"You hated him?" Arias asked.

"We all hated him," Lakinas said.

"Except for the people who went with him to the Scrapheap to get materials to fix the *Renegat*," Arias said.

"I don't know," Lakinas said. "I never talked to them."

"Why not?" Arias asked.

"Because they were Crowe's people," Lakinas said.

"And the only people with actual experience in running a ship like the *Renegat*, am I right?" Arias asked.

Lakinas shrugged one shoulder. "I suppose. I didn't investigate everyone's records."

Mukasey didn't like any of that. It made her nervous, and she wasn't exactly sure what Arias was going to do with it all. Especially since Arias antagonized her own witness.

"I have nothing further for this witness, Your Honor," Arias said. "But before we break for the evening, I would like to have my cross-examination of Admiral Gão. It will be brief."

"It better be," Chief Judge Kanberra said, although he didn't sound or look tired any longer. He seemed interested all over again.

The clerk recalled Admiral Gão to the stand. She walked as slowly toward it as Lakinas had when she left it. Except the ancient retired admiral seemed a lot more agile than the younger Lakinas.

"You're still under oath," Chief Judge Kanberra said to Gão.

She opened her mouth to say something, then apparently thought the better of it, and just nodded.

"I only have a few questions," Arias said. "Did you hear Ms. Lakinas's testimony and see the holo of Yusef Kabac?"

"Yes." Gão's voice was quiet. She seemed shaken.

"You testified that Captain Preemas had disobeyed your order to return. You also testified that it was possible he stole the *Renegat*," Arias said.

"Yes," Gão said.

"Under Fleet regulations," Arias said, "would a crew be justified in removing a captain in that circumstance?"

"It's a gray area," Gāo said. "But if the captain has been shown to be reckless and incompetent and the majority of his crew agree, then yes, he could have been removed. He should have been taken to the brig."

"But he wasn't," Arias said, "because, Nadim Crowe told you in his holo, they had to control the random and unpredictable trips into fold-space first."

"Yes," Gāo said.

Mukasey clenched her fists and placed them under the table. She wasn't going to be able to repair this.

"In the circumstance where a captain is deemed incompetent," Arias asked, "who takes control of the ship?"

"Regulations say that the first officer does, unless there is some pressing reason for him not to."

"You were also planning to make Nadim Crowe captain if you could, is that correct?" Arias asked.

"I considered it, yes," Gāo said.

"Would you have done it?" Arias asked.

"If there was a way to do so without bloodshed, yes," Gāo said.

Mukasey resisted the urge to close her eyes. She didn't want to listen to this anymore.

"So, after Captain Preemas's death," Arias said, "in your opinion, who was captain of the *Renegat?*"

"Nadim Crowe," Gāo said.

"According to Fleet regulations," Arias said, "when a crew throws a captain off a ship and takes that ship somewhere else, what is that called?"

Gāo lowered her head just a little. "It is one of the definitions of mutiny."

"Thank you," Arias said. "I'm done now, Your Honor."

The chief judge looked at Mukasey. "Redirect, counsellor?"

She almost asked *What's the point?* But she hung onto her professionalism just enough to stop that question from coming out of her mouth.

"No, Your Honor," she said.

"Then we're done for the day," he said, and gaveled the proceedings closed.

TWENTY-SEVEN

It took three more days for this never-ending case to actually end. Three more days of arguments and witnesses and attempts at repairing the damage.

But Mukasey could never find her footing.

If she were a different kind of attorney, she could have turned on her own clients, asked that Serpell and Kabac and maybe a few others get charged with the crime and the others be let go.

But she wasn't willing to try that. Besides, 193 people had committed one, maybe two, mutinies, and they decided *not* to commit one when the *Renegat* left Crowe and the others behind at the Scrapheap.

A first-year law student could argue that case and win.

Mukasey just had to survive and she did. Her closing argument focused on the defendants' amazing trip back to the Fleet against all odds, and she implied, because she didn't dare say, that they had been punished enough.

She knew that argument wouldn't hold, and it didn't.

The judges deliberated long enough to make it seem like they had spent time considering the evidence, but it had been clear from Gão's last statement that the case was over.

The judges came back with a unanimous verdict, something that rarely happened in a twelve-person tribunal. Usually one judge had a slightly different argument or a disagreement or some small nit to pick.

Not here.

The only gift the judges gave her was a small one. The ringleaders—Kabac, Serpell, and a few others—received life in prison. The rest received ten to twenty years. A few, those who had fought with Preemas, were banned from the Fleet. They would be sent to a rehabilitation center on the nearest Sector Base, before being exiled from any Fleet-established community.

Lakinas would be banned, after she received her court-ordered medical treatment. Others who had been denied similar treatment would get that as well.

The staggered sentences were probably fair, but she didn't care about that. The truth of it was that Mukasey had just suffered the worst defeat of her career.

She staggered out of court while the various guards were rounding up all of the defendants. They would lose their privileged quarters in tower six and be transported immediately to holding at the base of the starbase.

She didn't even get to say goodbye to them, not that she wanted to. She was certain they were as unwilling to deal with her as she was to deal with them.

The one thing she did decide at the end of this case was that she needed a life. She didn't even have real friends to go get drunk with, and she couldn't remember when she last had a lover.

That would change.

Maybe not even voluntarily. Because who was going to hire someone who was 1) willing to defend the undefendable and 2) who lost when doing it?

Then Mukasey squared her shoulders and made herself take a deep breath. She would give herself two full days of self-pity, maybe three.

After that, she was going to return to the land of the living. Because self-pity was one of the ways that the misnamed *Renegat* Renegades got into trouble.

All of them.

And she didn't want to mimic their behavior.

On anything.

TWENTY-EIGHT

Arias rested her head on her desk. The bullpen was quiet. She was tired, but she didn't mind as much as she usually did. This case was over, and she had won.

A hand slapped the desk beside her head, making her jump. She recognized that hand after weeks of watching it fiddle with tablets and tap restlessly on tables.

The Old Man.

"No sleeping!" he said. "We need to celebrate."

She lifted her head. The pile of tablets, coffee cups and odd bits of clothing (mostly suit jackets or tunics) threatened to tumble off the side of the desk. She caught the tablet stack, moved it, and then looked at him.

He didn't seem tired at all. He was grinning, his hair slightly mussed. He looked younger, like he always did when he smiled.

"We need to celebrate," he said.

"How do you propose we do that?" she asked.

"Great meal," he said. "Great booze. Lots of laughter."

One of the young lawyers—a new one, who had been hired during this case, whose name Arias hadn't learned yet—sat up on a nearby couch. Apparently he had heard the *no sleeping* command, and thought it applied to him.

"You're celebrating putting one hundred and ninety-three people away?" he asked.

"E-yup," the Old Man said, and then peered at the young lawyer. "You *are* in the prosecutor's office, you know."

"I know," the young lawyer said as if his life had ended, and flopped back down on the couch.

Arias smiled. She recognized lawyers like him. They either left the profession or became defense attorneys.

She forced herself out of the chair. Food would be good. Alcohol even better.

The Old Man was already threading his way through the desks. She had to hurry to catch up.

The smile had left the Old Man's face.

"Does it bother *you* that we are putting one hundred and ninety-three people away?" he asked.

"No," she said. "They are probably the worst group of people it has ever been my displeasure to encounter."

He laughed. "Yeah, they are that. But in their defense…"

She looked at him sharply. "Defense?"

"Yeah, defense. The one I was the most afraid of, actually, was the argument Mukasey never really made." He stopped near the door. "They were chosen because they were the worst. Why would they behave better as a collective than they had as individuals?"

Arias's breath caught. "You think that was a winning argument?"

The Old Man laughed. "In my hands, it would have been."

"But they—"

"Yeah, yeah," he said. "But really, who cares? It all happened one hundred years ago, in a Scrapheap so far away that we don't really understand where it is."

"Wow," Arias said. "That's very…nihilistic."

"Naw," he said, and started walking again.

He pulled open the door to the main office, the place she had just assumed she was returning to, now that this case was over.

"You know," he said, as if he were reading her thoughts. "That office is yours permanently."

"A private office?" she asked. "Really?"

"E-yup," he said, "but only if you promise to take over this entire department one day."

"Oh, wow, that's a condition." She was too tired to consider it right now. "Your argument—it probably wouldn't have succeeded in court."

"The key word in that sentence," he said as he stepped into the hallway, "is 'probably.'"

He was right. The key word was *probably*. And with the right combination of judges, a trial might have failed.

"That argument is not designed for trial," she said with a bit of wonder. "It casts enough doubt that a lesser prosecutor, one like that kid on the couch, would be willing to deal."

"Exactly," the Old Man said, clapping her on the back. She stumbled a little. "And that's the very last lesson of this case."

"You know," she said, moving slightly away from him, so he didn't try that back-clap again. "If I take over this department, I'll never be able to compete with your legend."

"Don't sell yourself short," he said. "You just won the biggest case we'd ever seen."

"You did," she said.

"*We* did," he said. "And that counts. But you're right. You'll never be me."

"Thank the universe for small miracles," she said. Then she grinned at him. "I'm picking the restaurant—and you're buying."

"Oh, no," he said. "This one's going on account. So we better make all that documentation worthwhile."

And, ultimately, they did.

A pulse-pounding new adventure as Boss has to make the dive of her life.

Get Thieves, the next exciting book in the series!

Pick up your copy of the next Diving novel *Thieves.*
Here's a sample chapter from the book.

THIEVES

I float outside the *Sove*, staring at the winking lights ahead of me. They look like a starfield, even though they are not. I am deep inside the Boneyard, a graveyard of old Fleet ships.

Three large ships float nearby, with smaller ships beside them. The ships appear to have been placed haphazardly with no real sense of order. They point in different directions, and some are what I would consider upside down, even though "up" and "down" have no real meaning in space.

I am out here alone, at my own insistence, so I can have time to contemplate what's before me. My environmental suit—a new version that Yash Zarlengo has redesigned for the umpteenth time—feels a little too tight. The new compression fabric that she used adheres to my skin, making me uncomfortable, even though I've been wearing this suit, or one of its cousins, for weeks now.

Unlike my older (and less effective, according to Yash) suit, this one aggressively reminds me that it exists. It monitors every part of my body, searching for the smallest physical change. The suit also monitors its own exterior, and—until I figured out how to shut it off—it would also notify me of each and every change.

I nearly died in this Boneyard several weeks ago. My diving companion, Elaine Seager, was badly injured. She's getting better, but the doctors back at the Lost Souls Corporation—and the consultants they've brought in—believe she will never recover completely.

That scared Yash who, as an engineer, believes that tech can and will save us from everything.

Elaine's injuries don't scare me as much. They just make me aware of the fact that my time in the universe is limited, and I need to work both harder and smarter to accomplish all that I want to do.

Such as figure out this silly Boneyard.

We have spent months here, diving vessels, testing them, and removing the viable ones. We take those vessels back to Lost Souls—or rather, someone on my team does.

I have found a haven in the Boneyard. I'm much more suited to diving vessels than I am to running a large corporation filled with diverse and interesting personalities. I prefer to be alone. I used to dive with a small team only after I had found the derelict vessels on my own. My single ship and I traveled everywhere, and I miss that solitude almost daily.

Which is probably why I'm out here by myself. The *Sove* is a Dignity Vessel or, rather, a DV-Class vessel, as my Fleet friends call these ships. The *Sove* is built for 500 crew along with their family members.

While we have a team of fifty to sixty depending on how many have gone back to Lost Souls and whether or not I've requested help in a certain area, we barely fill the *Sove's* tech requirements. We're always behind on personnel and training at Lost Souls, and it shows on missions like this.

The *Sove* is behind me. I'm aggressively tethered to it—at least three lines are hooked to my suit, two in the usual places that Yash had designed for tethers, and one attached to my old diving belt, along with some of my old equipment. The fact that I insist on that old belt bothers some on my team, but that doesn't stop me.

I do what I want because, no matter how hard I fight it, I am the one in charge.

The crew thinks I don't know that a bunch of them—maybe as many as half—are watching me out of the portals and on screens. Everyone worries about me, particularly after my near-death, but I feel curiously liberated.

I survived that traumatic experience. I'll survive others.

What I'm doing right now is only mildly dangerous. I'm not diving anything alone. I'm wearing the tethers because Mikk, who has been beside me for years, insisted upon it. I knew better than to argue; I would have insisted on it for him if our roles were reversed.

The suit's monitors are attached to all kinds of equipment inside. Every little detail is getting sent back to the *Sove*, including my physical readings, and the readings from the suit's exterior. The suit has four cameras which record the visuals around me from the front and back of my hood, as well as from the places where my right and left shoulders meet my arms. I can turn on cameras on the bottom of my boots and some underneath my wrists if I want to. Should something go seriously awry, the data stream will give my team clues as to why.

The suit picks up everything, except the one thing that sent me out here:

The music.

In this part of the Boneyard, I hear choral music in twenty-four-part harmony. It rises and falls in half-tones, crescendoing and decrescendoing in irregular, almost unpredictable intervals. I also hear other songs, farther away. Some sound like bells, ringing on a distant hillside. Others sound like old-fashioned piano music. And still others sound like human voices, melding in an atonal pattern.

The music doesn't really exist. It's simply the way that my senses perceive the *anacapa* energy levels mingling inside the Boneyard itself. If the music becomes too loud or too piercing, I know I'm in an energy field that's too strong for me, a field that might hurt or crush me.

Yash designed this suit to minimize the amount of energy that I can feel in my bones. That internal vibration is what causes these sounds. Not everyone feels these vibrations or "hears" them, as the case may be.

If the suit is actually working as designed, then my sensitivity is much higher than it has ever been. In my old suit, this level of sound would have been almost unbearable.

I haven't told Yash this, not since the incident. Yash is back at Lost

Souls, working on finding the Fleet, based on information we have brought back from this Boneyard. I haven't spoken to her in a long time.

I've spoken to Coop a lot, but I rarely tell him anything of substance. Jonathan "Coop" Cooper is the captain of the *Ivoire*, a DV-Class ship that found itself 5,000 years in its own future. He and I have a relationship that some would call casual, but which is pretty intimate, given who we both are. Or maybe given who I am.

Anyway, Coop isn't here either. He is currently helping Yash find the Fleet that they believe still exists.

I think it a fool's errand: even if they find the Fleet, it will be 5,000 years different. But this errand has focused them for years now, and it seems to give their lives meaning.

I cannot argue with that, any more than I can argue with the joy that I feel every time I enter an abandoned ship for the very first time.

Right now, though, it's not the abandoned ships around me that have caught my attention. It's that starfield which really isn't a starfield. It's something else entirely, and—most interestingly to me—it dims the sound of the music, especially when I get close.

I was close a few days ago, as I came out the rear hatch of an ancient orbiter. The sound was almost muted, which startled me. I have been in the Boneyard every single day for months, and the sound—while different, depending on where I am—has always been overwhelming.

So I've sent out the remaining five members of the Six, those who have the genetic marker that can enable them to survive in this kind of malfunctioning *anacapa* energy field and who are also familiar with the music. (Fleet members, who also have the gene, don't seem to hear the malfunction as music, which I find odd.)

The five all said that the music sounded different, but only one, Orlando Rea, described the difference as muted. I never prompted any of them by describing the sound, only asked them to get close to the starfield and see what they experienced.

That is what they reported.

We're doing more investigation—necessary investigation—but I wanted to see this for myself, out here, away from the constant barrage of questions from the others on the *Sove*. I also wanted to be as far as I could from the protection of the DV-class vessel.

I like floating in space, even though I probably shouldn't. I like having only the thin layer of an environmental suit between me and something so vast that I really have few words for it.

It doesn't quite feel like I'm in space, not when I'm floating here. The Boneyard is huge, larger than some planets I've visited. We'll never be able to dive all of the ships, which deeply disappoints me—not because I'm a completist, but because I feel like the history of the Fleet is here or at least part of it, and I adore history.

I want to learn everything I can.

It's as if I'm in an all-you-can-eat buffet, filled with foods I love, and I've been told I must eat my way out. I will never get to everything, and I'm overwhelmed half the time, and I'm still excited, each and every moment of each and every day.

We have worked deep into the Boneyard. We're following a trail that I've devised. I have a wish list of ships from Lost Souls. A variety of people compiled the list. Coop and Yash want certain kinds of Fleet vessels, mostly DV-Class, although Yash has started asking for others that I'd never heard of.

Ilona Blake, who runs Lost Souls because she can handle people oh so much better than I can, and because she actually cares about getting things done, has a completely different wish list. She wants defensive vessels as well as vessels we haven't seen before, because she wants to mine the technology for money.

She's monetized many of our discoveries already, turning them into tech that Lost Souls can develop and resell to various organizations within the Nine Planets Alliance.

I have been told to use my judgement, which apparently everyone still trusts, and I do use it. But I have a wish list of my own. I want to dive ships that have left their history intact, ships that still have information on their computers, ships that tell us as much about the past as they will help us with the future.

I find it ironic that I'm the one obsessed with the past, even as Yash and Coop search for information about what happened to the culture they left behind.

Or, Coop would say, that maybe it's not ironic. It's my love of history that led me to him and the *Ivoire*, the ship that brought them on that perilous journey from 5,000 years ago to now. They arrived over five years ago, and are still getting their footing.

I'm not sure I ever would.

Mikk pings me.

"What are you seeing?" he asks, and I smile. He knows what I'm seeing. He can see it too.

I've just been silent too long for his tastes. I'm not even sure I've moved.

"I'll tell you when I get back," I say.

This excursion of mine—which isn't a dive, really, although that's what we called it back on the ship—isn't timed. Usually we time any exploration a crew member makes outside the ship. I usually insist on that.

The missions have a duration, one that we adhere to, and we have goals that we have to meet on our journey, whatever it is.

But this isn't a journey. It's just an observation, and I never placed a timeline on it.

I hit the team with this trip so fast that no one thought to suggest a timeline either.

Which is probably making Mikk nervous.

It would have made me nervous, if he had been out here by himself.

I glance at the timer which I have running in the clear part of my hood, beneath my left eye. Running the timer is a force of habit. I start it when I emerge from the airlock, and shut down the timer the moment I return.

I've been here for less than fifteen minutes. But I haven't done anything dramatic, which is probably bothering him.

I have moved to the very edge of the tethers, which places me as close to the starfield as I can get.

There is no atmosphere in the Boneyard, even though there are some energy cross currents. Something—we don't know what, exactly—holds the ships and the ship parts scattered throughout this gigantic place in exact position. Even when we board the smaller ships, our movement makes no difference in that placement.

Which led me to believe, initially anyway, that the starfield was something else entirely—a bit of energy, tiny bits of ships that reflect some of the ambient light in this place. To be honest, I didn't pay much attention to the starfield when I first saw it, because we have seen so many strange things since we started working the Boneyard.

In addition to intact ships that have been stored here, the Fleet also stored ship parts and destroyed bits of ships. Sometimes the parts are scattered around the ships, and sometimes they aren't. Sometimes parts of a certain type congregate together as if someone designed that section of the Boneyard that way.

Perhaps someone had.

But the deeper we've gotten into the Boneyard, the more I think that we're seeing different intelligences at play in the way everything is organized.

The placement of ships along the edge, where we first entered the Boneyard, is haphazard at best. They seem tossed in, left wherever they were placed with no thought of leaving pathways for other ships to get past them. The extra ship parts and remains of damaged ships are tossed in as well, sometimes so close to nearby ships that we can't get between them.

Farther in, ship parts have been placed with similar parts. Smaller ships are lined up in rows, their noses pointing in the same direction. Larger ships are equidistant from each other, and all facing the same direction as well.

Still farther in, undamaged ships rest next to each other, while damaged ships squeeze into a smaller space. In that section of the Boneyard, there are no ship parts at all.

Here, where we're currently working, the ships form necklaces around the starfield. The pattern seems different. Large ship, small ship, ship part, almost like multi-sized beads. The necklaces (as we've started to call them) run up, down, around, and diagonally. They form an actual curtain around this area, one that made the starfield impossible to see as a field when we were not as deep into the Boneyard.

Only in the last week did I even see the field. At that point, I thought it *was* a starfield, viewed through some kind of barrier. I didn't think much about it. We were focused on the ships we were diving, not on what was ahead of us.

If someone had asked me (and no one had), I would have said that the starfield was a gap in the Boneyard, or we had reached one of the edges earlier than we expected.

But assumptions always bother me. I learned early in my diving career that assumptions lead to mistakes. So I double-checked myself, first with my own scans and then with the help of others on the crew.

Our scans showed we were deep in the Boneyard and had a long way to go in all directions if we wanted to travel out of it on regular power. We weren't even in the center of the Boneyard. In fact, we were so far away from the center that it would take us years at the pace we are currently working to get to the center.

We are moving forward (or what we consider to be forward) into the Boneyard, using the *Sove's* regular drive. We let ourselves through the security field on the outside of the Boneyard, using ancient codes that still worked.

But for the rest of our work—getting the ships back to Lost Souls, for example—we use the ships' *anacapa* drives, after one of our engineers ensures that the drives are actually working. The drives travel across a fold in space—at least, that's how Yash explains it—covering a tremendous amount of distance in minutes instead of years.

We have to be very careful when we use *anacapa* drives inside the Boneyard. Yash worries (and she has gotten me to worry) that the wrong type of *anacapa* energy might cause some kind of chain reaction in here, something that might send a bunch of ships into foldspace, or worse (or maybe not worse) make the ships explode.

It's the *anacapa* energy that has me bothered. We can measure it. There is all kinds of what I call rogue *anacapa* energy throughout the Boneyard, leaking from the ships with working drives. Some of the energy is exactly as we would expect from a dormant drive—just a low-level reading, when we get close enough to the ship to experience it.

But a lot of the energy is spiky and random—filled with power sometimes, and without much at other times. Sometimes the energy seems corrupted, and other times it gives off readings that our sensors make no sense of.

I record all of it—the *Sove* records all of it—but I don't send much of it back to Lost Souls. Technically, Ilona can't cancel this mission, but she can make it almost impossible for me to run the mission. She can take away supplies or not authorize personnel.

And Yash, in particular, would monitor what happens in the Boneyard and have an opinion about it, one Ilona would listen to.

I'm not giving them the ability to have an opinion.

Not yet, anyway.

But I might, if I can't figure out this starfield.

Because the energy readings around it here, near these carefully placed ships, is different. Not in the types of readings, which vary from day to day and hour to hour in every section of the Boneyard we've traveled through.

But in the *level* of the readings.

There's less energy here around these carefully placed ships. They seem to have working *anacapa* drives. Even the small ships have *anacapa* drives, and that's unusual. The Fleet stopped outfitting small ships with *anacapa* drives sometime before Yash and Coop were born.

The random *anacapa* energy, the kind that indicates a deteriorating or damaged drive, is almost nonexistent, at least the closer we get to that starfield.

Then Mikk and I turned our attention to the starfield, and what was behind it. According to our scans, more ships lie behind that starfield curtain, all of them in the same neat rows that are in front of it.

Our scans didn't get the right level of energy readings, though, for that number of ships, at least, depending on what we had seen before in the Boneyard. (And, I know, I can't really depend on that, because each section of the Boneyard has been different so far.)

Still, the differences afforded me the time to study the field. And what I learned shook me. I discovered that I can take the images of those ships *outside* the starfield, and place them on top of the images of the ships *inside* the starfield, and they match exactly.

Either the Fleet or its minders got *really* precise, or they created some kind of ghost scan.

No matter which scanner I use, no matter how I calibrate our instruments on the *Sove*, I get that ghost scan reading.

And I've started to suspect that the scan will show up on any Fleet equipment.

I want to use a different vessel to scan that starfield, some vessel not made by the Fleet. Unfortunately, we don't have any with us.

And we did that deliberately. This Boneyard has fired on non-Fleet ships in the past.

Even my environmental suit, with its limited scanning capability, was built with Fleet tech. But I brought some non-Fleet tech with me on my old diving belt. Besides my ancient diving knife, which I recovered from one of my old diving partners, Karl, after his tragic death, I carry a few tiny probes and three small scanners of different vintages.

I pluck the one of those old scanners off my belt. This scanner is the "newest" of the three, although I wouldn't exactly call it new. It's also the least sophisticated.

The scanner fits nicely in my hand. I had forgotten how malleable my old tech was. It feels like an old friend, one I haven't given enough thought to over the decades, one I forgot that I loved.

I hold the scanner in front of my belly, out of the view of any of the cameras on my suit. As long as I only move my eyes to look at the scanner, not my entire head.

I don't want someone to yank me back to the *Sove* in a great panic before I have a chance to use the scanner.

Using the scanner is my biggest risk. If the Boneyard hates *all* non-Fleet tech, then there is a very good chance the Boneyard will fire on me.

And that will be the end of me.

But I'm gambling that there's lots of small, random, non-Fleet tech in this Boneyard. Some of that non-Fleet tech might be in the cargo holds of the old ships around me; other parts might be grafted onto ships after some emergency on some distant planet.

I'm gambling that the Boneyard only objects to active, working, non-Fleet ships, the kind that might want to steal ships from the Boneyard itself.

Like we are.

A fact I do my best to ignore.

Someone left these ships in the Boneyard. They're protected by a forcefield that we are able to get through because we know the codes and we have a Fleet vessel, apparently of the right vintage.

But that someone might return for these ships.

Coop believes that the Fleet has stored the ships in the Boneyard because it didn't know what else to do with them. Yash agrees with a slight difference; she thinks the ships were stored here so that they could be used by traveling Fleet vessels like Security Class ships that sometimes have to go backwards.

I've even heard a few members of the *Ivoire* crew say that they believed the ships were here in case some Fleet vessel got stuck in foldspace and needed them, but I think that's more of a reflection on the problems the *Ivoire* had than it is anything that the Fleet tried to create with this Boneyard.

The Boneyard is a mystery to me, and as I do with all mysteries that I find in space, I'm exploring it.

The fact that I'm removing ships from it at the same time makes me a lot more nervous than I want to admit.

Until this last year, I was never the kind of wreck diver who plundered the abandoned ships that I found. I had some of my divers report the ancient abandoned ships. A few even claimed them, so that they would get the wealth found on the ships. And one tried to get me in trouble with the Enterran Empire (back when I lived there), by claiming that I was trying to co-opt stealth tech (which turns out to be *anacapa* technology).

But now I have found a literal planet-sized graveyard of abandoned ships, and I am taking some back to my own corporation, for personal use, and I feel guilty about it.

Guilty, and worried, and afraid we'll get caught.

By whom, I have no idea, since everything we've found in this Boneyard so far points to the fact that no one—not outside ships, not the Fleet itself—has been inside this Boneyard in at least a thousand years, maybe more.

We can't be certain, because we can't cover the entire area of the Boneyard. But we've found even more information on the ships we've sent back. Many of the ships had a baseline program running, even though the ships were powered down. That program monitored every contact the ships had, every unusual thing that happened around them while they were powered down. Some even had systems that edited the information into highlights, marked with the year something occurred.

We have real-time video and information about when other ships were added to the Boneyard, and I'm sure that Yash is pulling information from that in her quest to find the Fleet.

What I watched seemed straightforward. I hadn't seen anything that seemed out of the ordinary. The ships arrived, the skeleton team that brought them would leave, usually on a small ship, and then the larger ship would remain powered down. Occasionally it would wake up when other ships or ship parts were placed near it.

And then it would sleep again.

Maybe we just hadn't hit the exciting part of the Boneyard yet.

And every time I have had that thought of late, I find my mind drifting to that starfield. Maybe what's behind it is the exciting part of the Boneyard.

Maybe that's why I'm out here.

I'm ready to find out.

I raise the scanner so it's directly in my line of sight. Images of the scanner have just gone back to the *Sove.* Right now, a handful of people, staring out those portals or looking at the feed, have gasped, stunned that I'm holding something they don't recognize.

I'm sure a few of them are panicked, worried that I've gone off some kind of deep end.

Where did she get that? Why is she holding it? What the hell is she doing?

I smile at the imagined words, and brace myself for Mikk's voice, but he doesn't say anything.

He doesn't have the right to. He's the one who attached my tethers. He saw the belt. He commented on the knife.

Are you sure you should take Karl's knife? Mikk asked. He's an old spacer like me, and we're both just a bit more superstitious than we probably should be.

The sentence that went unsaid was *He died wearing it, you know.*

Technically, he didn't, though. Technically, he had unhooked his belt with all of his safety equipment, backup breathers, and his knife—or maybe it had all come undone in the strange time field he had found himself in back at the place the Enterran Empire and the Nine Planets call The Room of Lost Souls, and the *Ivoire* crew calls Starbase Kappa.

But Mikk is correct about one thing: Karl had the knife with him on the mission that killed him.

I know that. After Karl died, I started carrying the knife on some dangerous missions to honor him, and to help myself remember the risks that we take.

I had stopped doing that over the years.

But I've wanted the knife beside me on my dives since I got injured. I don't have lingering effects—at least I don't have noticeable ones—from that near-death incident, and I don't want to forget it.

The knife is a reminder to me to be careful as much as it is a talisman.

Only I didn't explain that to Mikk. Instead I said, *I'm taking it.*

He glanced down at my belt and shook his head slightly. There is absolutely no way that he missed the fact that I was carrying other equipment too.

He didn't say anything about it, though. He knows me very well. He knows that I am unorthodox still, despite the corporation, the large operations, the various businesses I run.

He knows I like to take risks.

And, I like to believe, that he understands them.

I take a deep breath of the filtered air, conscious of the fact that my heart rate has increased. I'm sure someone inside the *Sove* has noted that as well. I'm sure they're having serious conversations about what to do with me right now.

And the moment I have that thought, I shut it down.

I need to concentrate, and I don't need anyone else in the middle of my work.

I squeeze the scanner. Red rays of light reflect off a nearby ship. The scanner is so old that it actually uses light to show which side is the functioning side, just in case someone can't figure it out from the grip.

I move the scanner from the right side of my body to the left. Then I move the scanner up and down.

I'm sending information back to the *Sove*, but not in the usual way. The information goes to me, to my quarters, to some equipment I set up there.

If he's smart, if he planned for this, then Mikk will be able to piggyback off the signal and get the same information.

But I hadn't instructed him to do that, so I'm not going to expect it of him. Mikk is good, but he can't always read my mind.

I try not to expect him to.

I scan as much of the area before me as I can without letting go of the scanner. I had initially thought of sending some of the old non-Fleet probes to the starfield, and then ruled that out. They were mobile and active; something inside that field or whatever generated that field might consider the probe some type of weapon.

Or might recognize it as non-Fleet tech and therefore consider it hostile.

It might be another way of getting me shot.

I'm not worried about the Boneyard attacking the scanner. My gloved hand covers most of it. Only the front of the scanner is pointed at the starfield, and I am quite far away from it. At least three DV-Class ship lengths away, maybe more.

The scanner vibrates in my hand, a signal that the scanner has gathered all the information it can from the area I pointed it at. I learned a long time ago, with this scanner, that it doesn't handle small differences well. So it really doesn't matter if I hold the scanner up for ten minutes or fifty. If it scans an area at one time, scanning that same area later won't give me any different information.

So, I squeeze the scanner, shutting down the scan function. Then I shut the scanner off, and tuck it back into its place on my belt. Then I grab another scanner, one that's a bit fussier, and turn it on.

I had set the controls back on the *Sove*, so that I wouldn't have to do any programming out here, and I'm grateful for that now. Because my internal clock tells me I've been out here too long.

If I were running a dive from inside the *Sove*, I would tell my diver it was time to come back to the ship.

Mikk hasn't said that yet, but that's probably due to the fact that I'm the one on this dive, not some member of our crew.

I have to press my gloved thumb against the side of the scanner to start the scan. I hold the scanner up, like I did with the last one, and press the scanner's side. There's no old-fashioned red light, nothing except a quiet beep inside my hood to tell me that the scanner is working.

And then, in a small square on the lower right of my faceplate, an image shows up. The image is blurry at first, and not at all what I expect.

I had thought I would see reflected light, or the ships that had shown up in the *Sove's* scans, bizarrely lined up like the ships outside the field.

But I hadn't expected the blur.

I had set this scanner to send me the actual visuals. The telemetry, the readings in every different form, are being sent, as with the last scanner, back to Mikk and to my quarters.

It takes me a moment to remember how this scanner works in the wild. I press my thumb against it again, which sets the scan at maximum. I won't run it at maximum for long, because this scanner has a weird battery glitch that has always irritated me about it. But I want to see that visual one more time.

As the scanner recalibrates, I catch the sound of my own breathing. It's ragged. My heart rate has probably gone up again, and I'm sure Mikk won't like that. Nor will anyone else.

I force myself to breath slower. The filtered air tastes dry, almost flat. I'm pushing this dive to its edges, and I know that.

The visual winks out for a second and then returns, stronger and clearer. What I had taken to be a blur isn't. It's an actual barrier that I can't see past. As I watch it, lights rotate through it.

What I had thought was the winking of a light through atmosphere, the way that starlight seems to wink to someone on a planet below, is actually faint lights appearing at intervals on that barrier. It's some way of letting someone—something—us, maybe—know that the barrier is both there and working.

The visual part of the scanner doesn't show any ships at all. It shows nothing past that barrier.

"That's enough, Boss." Mikk's voice is so loud that it startles me. I jump. I wish I could take back the startle reaction: it means I'm not paying enough attention to everything around me. Only to that scan.

Then he says the words I have been expecting for at least twenty minutes. "I'm calling an end to this dive. Right now."

I open my mouth to protest, then close it. I know he's right. I also know that I set an example for the crew with everything that I do.

And I'm always the one who insists on procedure. I'm the one who tells each diver they have to listen to their monitor. I'm the one who stresses over and over again that failing to follow these rules could lead to death.

But oh, do I understand the temptation to ignore them. Especially right now.

Especially as my eye catches a glimpse of something on that visual. It's a white trail, almost as if some ship were traveling by, venting chemicals against the blackness of space.

That white trail leads into the barrier.

I raise my gaze just enough to look at what still seems like a starfield to me. The white trail looks like the edges of a galaxy, or maybe an asteroid belt, at least from this distance.

I glance at the visual again, and realize that what the scanner shows is something more akin to a comet tail.

A mystery. An enigma. Mysteries and enigmas hook me every time.

"Boss." Mikk sounds fierce.

I haven't answered him, which is probably scaring the heck out of him, even though he can see from my suit readings that I'm still alive.

"Yeah," I say curtly. Then I add, because I can't stop myself, "This is fascinating."

"I don't care," he says. "You're coming back to the ship."

I sigh, probably audibly enough that anyone monitoring this dive can hear me.

"Yeah," I say again. Then I move the scanner right to left, as I did with the previous scanner, only faster than I probably should have. "I'm coming."

I feel like a recalcitrant child. I'm probably acting a bit like one too. I shut off the scanner. That small square image vanishes, and I actually miss it.

I'm learning something, and whenever I do that, I feel alive.

I replace the scanner on my belt, then turn to my left, careful not to get entangled in my tethers.

I grab one of them, and use it to pull myself back to the *Sove*.

I resist the urge to look over my shoulder. I almost feel as though if I do, I will be tempting fate, preventing myself from traveling back to the ship.

We've found—I've found—yet another mystery inside this Boneyard—and it has me intrigued.

Follow Kris on BookBub!

I value honest feedback, and would love to hear your opinion in a review, if you're so inclined, on your favorite book retailer's site.

Be the first to know!

Just sign up for the Kristine Kathryn Rusch newsletter, and keep up with the latest news, releases and so much more—even the occasional giveaway.

So, what are you waiting for? To sign up go to kristinekathrynrusch.com.

But wait! There's more. Sign up for the WMG Publishing newsletter, too, and get the latest news and releases from all of the WMG authors and lines, including Kristine Grayson, Kris Nelscott, Dean Wesley Smith, *Pulphouse Fiction Magazine, Smith's Monthly,* and so much more.

To sign up go to wmgpublishing.com.

ABOUT THE AUTHOR

New York Times bestselling author Kristine Kathryn Rusch writes in almost every genre. Generally, she uses her real name (Rusch) for most of her writing. Under that name, she publishes bestselling science fiction and fantasy, award-winning mysteries, acclaimed mainstream fiction, controversial nonfiction, and the occasional romance. Her novels have made bestseller lists around the world and her short fiction has appeared in eighteen best of the year collections. She has won more than twenty-five awards for her fiction, including the Hugo, *Le Prix Imaginales*, the *Asimov's* Readers Choice award, and the *Ellery Queen Mystery Magazine* Readers Choice Award.

Publications from *The Chicago Tribune* to *Booklist* have included her Kris Nelscott mystery novels in their top-ten-best mystery novels of the year. The Nelscott books have received nominations for almost every award in the mystery field, including the best novel Edgar Award, and the Shamus Award.

She writes goofy romance novels as award-winner Kristine Grayson.

She also edits. Beginning with work at the innovative publishing company, Pulphouse, followed by her award-winning tenure at *The Magazine of Fantasy & Science Fiction*, she took fifteen years off before returning to editing with the original anthology series *Fiction River*, published by WMG Publishing. She acts as series editor with her husband, writer Dean Wesley Smith, and edits at least two anthologies in the series per year on her own.

To keep up with everything she does, go to kriswrites.com and sign up for her newsletter. To track her many pen names and series, see their individual websites (krisnelscott.com, kristinegrayson.com, retrievalartist.com, divingintothewreck.com, pulphouse.com).

facebook.com/kristinekathrynruschwriter
bookbub.com/authors/kristine-kathryn-rusch
patreon.com/kristinekathrynrusch

www.ingramcontent.com/pod-product-compliance
Lightning Source LLC
Chambersburg PA
CBHW020611310726
48979CB00008B/1437/J

* 9 7 8 1 5 6 1 4 6 8 7 2 0 *